125 West St

by
Willie Egan

125 West St
By Willie Egan
Published in 2025

A Note on the Author

Willie Egan has always loved writing, despite being told as a young man by one of his religious mentors, "I worry about people who always want to be writing. It has long been my view that writers are not happy people, not happy in or with the world that the Lord in his goodness has given them. So they try to create an alternative world in their head through their writing. Alas, this fantasy world also fails to bring the promised happiness, so they end up in a kind of discontented limbo between the real world and the one in their heads."

He's had five of his original plays produced on stage in Kilkenny's Watergate Theatre. This is his first attempt at writing a novel. Will it be his last? You the reader hold the answer to that particular question. He sees this book – drawing on the words of Kris Kristofferson – "…as a walking contradiction, partly truth and partly fiction, taking every wrong direction on its lonely way back home." (The Pilgrim)

Willie has run his own private practice talk-therapy clinic in Kilkenny for more than twenty-five years, working mostly with teenagers who find life difficult for whatever reason. There's a chapter in this book which explains his raison d'être for same. He was somewhat of a "late vocation" to this particular profession, having "served his time" in a variety of sales positions and working in the caring profession.

Dedication

This book is dedicated to the memory of the founder-member of PCI College, Dublin, who, at a key time of my life, encouraged me, saw something in me that I and others perhaps failed to see. He inspired me to greater things and thereby ensured I would follow the path destined for me.

Constantly encouraging my creative side, he came to see all of my self-written plays in Kilkenny's Watergate Theatre and used the vast college network to encourage others to do the same. Not alone encouraging me, he very much influenced and shaped the person who I became, personally and professionally.

For that, I am eternally indebted to his memory.

That man was Liam McCarthy, whose generosity, influence and integrity I should not – could not – and will not – ever forget.

My tribute poem to Liam within this book sums up how I felt then, how I feel now and how I will always feel.

Willie Egan

"And some say love is holding on
And some say letting go
And some say love is everything
And some say they don't know"

(John Denver – Perhaps Love)

...walking the streets in the rain...

A brief look outside confirms that it's a dark, cold and wet April morning in Dunstable, England. The year is 1986. It's 8.15am and a second glance tells Charlie McCann that the traffic is already building on the busy street outside the front door. Having checked that his daughter's anorak is properly secured in the manner her mother Vera would have insisted on, he takes his nine-year-old daughter Mary Elizabeth's hand and closes the door of 125 West St behind them.

A few months short of his thirty-fourth birthday, Charlie's default personality is that of a calm man, but default personalities tend to have a shadow side when stressed. A little over six feet tall with sandy blonde hair, broad shoulders and pale blue eyes, he has about him all the traits and manners of a man, blended with the inquisitiveness and excitement of a boy. It's that particular combination which enabled him to be a good writer of plays back in his native Ireland. But in this particular moment in time, this is not a play, and the creative calm man is nowhere to be seen as he attempts to deal with an increasingly difficult situation.

Marianne, the main reason for his moving to Dunstable with his daughter a little over four weeks ago, left for work some time earlier.

Mary Elizabeth is tall for her nine years, her long blond hair tied with a neat bow. Under normal circumstances, Mary Elizabeth's wonder seems to know no bounds and her caring nature makes it easy for her to make friends. Being a morning person, she usually sees every day as an adventure, her bright blue eyes dancing every time she smiles. But this situation is not usual and when stressed, those eyes tend to change to a shade of grey as her pretty little face reflects what she is feeling. This is one of those mornings.

As they begin their morning walk to her new school, Charlie and Mary Elizabeth are equally unhappy for overlapping but significantly distinct reasons. For the child, it is the massive move from a small primary school in a rural South East Ireland village to a busy suburban junior school in Dunstable, which seems to the child to have more classrooms than there were pupils back home. For Charlie, his child's unease is also his, but for him there are bigger issues at play.

He has slept little, disturbed by Mary Elizabeth's comments the previous night.

'When are we going home, Daddy?'

Charlie had continued reading her bedtime story, hoping she might forget.

'You said we were only coming over here to see your friend for a few days.'

At which point he looked to the ceiling, hoping for some kind of inspiration which never came.

He vaguely muttered unconvincingly, 'Soon, pet, soon.'

'Do you promise?'

Charlie knew his history on keeping promises was not something to be proud of, but he decided this was not the time to fix that.

'Yes, pet.'

False or not, with the comfort of that promise, the child fell asleep.

But that was last night and this is this morning.

'You're hurting my hand and you're walking really fast,' Mary Elizabeth says crossly, while looking straight ahead.

Now, if there is one thing that could hurt Charlie more than his father's disapproval, it would be the mere hint of Mary Elizabeth's not being happy with him. As he guiltily adjusts both his grip and his stride, he realises that he is not managing the situation over here very well at all.

His daughter's next comment doesn't help.

'I don't like this school. When am I going back to my old school?'

He repeats his awkward reassurances that she will be going home soon, but his words are beginning to sound increasingly hollow, even to himself. He knows it, and he senses that she knows it, which breaks his heart.

Maybe I'm not cut out for this new life after all, he thinks to himself, and neither is my daughter. There is love that *feels* right and there's love that *is* right, and as he continues to walk his child to a place neither she nor he any longer wants, he finds himself experiencing a huge lesson in the very real gap between the two.

He is comforted to realise he has no work today, so he will have time to possibly rethink this whole operation on his own.

What Charlie does not know in this precise moment is that in the few short minutes it will take them to reach the school gate, fate will lend a significant hand. Charlie's lies to his child will become the truth in a manner he could not have envisaged.

One minute he is walking his child to a school she doesn't like in the cold rain, thinking this can't get any worse.

The next minute, it has gotten worse. There is a sudden blaring of car horns accompanied by the sound of screeching tyres as two cars in convoy pull up alongside him, causing traffic and pedestrian mayhem. Charlie tries to adjust his mind to whatever seems to be going on. Not for a second does he think it has anything to do with him.

But that quickly changes when three hooded men jump out of the two cars simultaneously in a well-rehearsed movement. The apparent ringleader is shouting at him to let go of the child in a strikingly identifiable accent, as the other two push him against a garden wall. The ringleader delivers a well-aimed blow to his solar plexus which disables him.

Because of the paralysing effect of pain and fear, Charlie finds he is unable to let go of his daughter's hand.

As the child screams in terror, his grip is finally broken and the child is passed to a fourth person, equally disguised, who had remained in the rear seat of the second car. The initial sound of screeching tyres and loud voices is being replaced by the equally frightening noise of what seems to Charlie to be a thousand drivers repeatedly blowing their horns in some kind of non-musical orchestral manoeuvre.

Unperturbed, the remaining three masked enforcers calmly join their drivers as both cars speed off in convoy, using the same scare tactics of repeated car horns and reckless driving on the footpath.

Charlie knows that the enforced physical separation of his daughter's hand from his will forever haunt him. He fears it may be a metaphor for their really close relationship being torn apart for life due to his utter stupidity and cruelty in having placed her in such danger in the first place. The other triggering image is that of her crying face as she tries to call out to him through the car's rear window before being dragged back into the car, remarkably similar to a graphic scene from his own young life when he was the one crying, looking out a car rear window.

Then in a flash they are gone, as a dazed Charlie almost in slow motion sinks to a squatting position alongside the low garden wall. His brain is trying to come to terms with what has just happened, while the traumatic turmoil of the last few minutes is eerily replaced by the equally deafening sound of silence.

Charlie enters a space of spatial disorientation, the natural anaesthetic of numbness, to protect his very survival from the shockwaves that could otherwise derail it completely. His mind is gradually and painfully getting pierced from all angles by intense flashing images of what has just happened, as his heart is feeling shattered. This state of disorientation is being assisted by an equally default state of denial, as if the past few minutes have just been part of some bad dream, where he and his daughter are still safe in their bed, waiting for the alarm to go off.

But that respite is brief as some conscientious passersby, who have witnessed the event, come to check on him. One phones the police as he proudly tells Charlie that he got the number of one of the cars, a Ford Capri 2.8i. At that, the passersby leave one by one.

Charlie suddenly finds himself alone, but not for long, as a police car arrives with sirens and flashing lights, which at this point seem more disturbing to Charlie than the earlier incident. In his thirty-four years of life to date in his native Ireland, Charlie has never experienced the inside of either a Garda car or a Garda Station. He is only in Dunstable a few short weeks and already he realises that he can view his sheltered life back in Ireland through the lens of nostalgia.

Within a matter of minutes, he finds himself in Dunstable Police Station being examined by a doctor. Having established there are no serious physical injuries, he is informed the doctor will return later to check for signs of delayed shock. He is moved to a different room, one with lots of cameras, where he is joined by two police officers who invite him to make a full statement of all that has happened since he left 125 West St that morning.

After he has falteringly recounted his memories of the school-walk, the questions begin.

'Is the child yours? Where is the child's mother? How long have you and the child been in Dunstable? On what business? Do you have ID on you? Have you a photograph of your daughter on you? Have you any idea who might have snatched the child and why?'

Even in his disorientated state, Charlie understands the complex dilemma facing the police. They have to treat the assault on him as a criminal offence in itself, while also trying to establish if someone has just kidnapped his daughter, or if she in fact has been kidnapped by him from

5

her home in Ireland in the first place. And he equally knows he is in the throes of an ethical dilemma himself. Does he really want the police to chase these guys down and thereby deprive his child of her earnest wish to get back home?

After a while, a detective joins them.

'We have just received an anonymous call from a phone-box in South East Ireland in which a woman has relayed that the child taken this morning is safe. That was all she was willing to say, other than to tell us the child's date of birth and certain other information about her that only someone close to her could know. So, can you please confirm the child's date of birth for us?'

'Seventeenth of May, 1977,' he replies.

After asking him a few more questions, and receiving answers, the detective adds, 'We are relatively satisfied as to the bone fides of the call and the caller, but what happened this morning constitutes a serious crime and we will be using all available resources to ensure that the full rigour of British Law is applied.'

The questioning continues.

'Based on the detail of that phone call, would you have any better idea as to who the anonymous caller might be, or who the people who carried out the snatch might be?'

To which Charlie pleads ignorance.

'Do you believe the child's mother is involved?'

Again, Charlie claims to have no idea.

'Oh, come on, Mr McCann, surely you couldn't have taken your child over here from Ireland without upsetting a lot of people, people who would want her back.'

Fortuitously for Charlie, a female detective comes into the room precisely at that moment to say the car registration plate as taken down by the passerby is from a stolen vehicle. Charlie tries not to show his relief at that news. Inside, he feels it was Mary Elizabeth's aunt, Ailish, who made that call. The police say they will need to contact the child's mother, but on Charlie's informing them that his former home doesn't have a landline, they tell him they will be in touch with his local Garda Station back home to confirm Charlie's story and to update them on the developing situation.

'We are actively monitoring all air and sea ports. Is there anything else you can add to help us?

Charlie shakes his head. Just then the doctor returns for further examinations and confirms there are no obvious signs of delayed emotional trauma or psychological damage.

He's told he's free to go but given a list of conditions.

'If you hear anything more about the events of this morning, you must let us know immediately. If you hear over the coming days that the child is back in Ireland, you must let us know.' Charlie nods in agreement but before he leaves, one of the detectives observes, 'You know more than you're saying, Mr McCann.'

The resulting silence helps neither party.

…that's the way dreams are…

Ruffled by the final hypothesis put to him in the police station, Charlie politely declines their offer to bring him home. Besides, he's tired, his head is fried, his heart is in bits, and his body's aching like it's been run over at least twice by both of the cars that took his child. Despite the relentless cold rain, he needs fresh air and the space in which to breathe it. He's no stranger to difficult moments in his life, but nothing like this. And he knows with great certainty that if part one of the day's nightmare has ended, part two is waiting for him.

He can feel the cold chains, referred to in the title of one of his plays, *Chains of Freedom*, wrapping themselves tightly around him, as he makes his weary way back to the house. He suddenly can clearly see this town is not the city of dreams it had promised to be. With this turn of events there will be no future for him here. Perhaps it was never meant to be. Why and how did he get it so wrong? He's relieved that he will be alone at least for a few hours. He needs time to get his head around all that has happened and knows he will have to explain the events of this morning to Marianne, and that will require rehearsing.

As he turns the key in 125 West St, with strikingly painful memories of his child screaming at him from every space she's sat, stood, did her homework in or watched TV from, the phone rings. It's probably Marianne but he chooses to let it ring out. The news he has for her will be better delivered face-to-face.

Besides, it only reminds him that it had been Mary Elizabeth using that same phone a week previously that led to the exposure of their whereabouts. In perhaps a state of loneliness, and with no way of contacting her mother, she had decided to reach out to her cousin back home, which unlike his own home, had a house phone. Aged just nine,

8

she had somehow figured out from the British telephone directory on the table how to dial an Irish number.

Of course, when the cousin's mother Ailish realised who was on the phone she immediately took over the call and got all the details she needed from the innocent child, who seemed to sense that might cause trouble, so she confessed all to Charlie when he came home from work that evening and expected him to be mad. But how could he be, having been the very architect of her homesickness? He had decided not to share that information with Marianne. In the light of this morning's events, that probably was his first mistake. After the child's sharing of that call, Charlie secretly knew that their days of being left alone were possibly numbered. He now knows he was right.

He knows that his immediate task now is to dial the same number the child had called a week earlier. His hand shaking, he dials the number, which is answered by Ailish, whom he strongly suspects is the person who had spoken to the police earlier.

Her curt greeting, once she hears his voice, is, 'You have some neck calling here, when you hadn't called as much as once during the last four weeks to reassure someone that the child was ok.'

Ailish is five years older than Charlie's wife, Vera. A tall, striking-looking woman with short brown hair, Ailish is still unmarried and living with their mother, Alice. Apparently she had been engaged a few years before Charlie met Vera, but he was quickly told there was to be no mention of it.

'She was with me. Of course she was ok,' he replies, getting the strength from somewhere.

'Have you any idea of the torture you put everyone here through, especially my sister Vera who has been out of her mind without her only child?'

That statement hits Charlie so hard that she has to repeat another curt *Hello* to regain his focus.

'Is Mary Elizabeth okay?' he finally asks in an attempt to recover his composure.

'She is now, no thanks to you, and please God the poor child will be back in her own home tomorrow, a place from which she should never have been taken. And I'm telling you now that if you do anything to stop it, your wife will never forgive you, I will never forgive you and Mary Elizabeth will never forgive you. Do you hear me?'

After his chat with his daughter last night and this morning, Charlie knows there's truth in what she says, particularly in the last piece of her statement.

He then anxiously enquires, 'Does Mary Elizabeth know anyone in that car?'

'After what you've done, you don't deserve to know, but yes, there is someone she will recognise. I made sure of that, but I'm not telling you who it is. She or he was also well disguised, but once in the car they would have immediately identified themselves to the child.'

If that brings relief to Charlie, it is short lived.

'Is there another woman involved?'

Charlie's silence on the subject seems to act as a spur.

'There's no point in denying it. We will shortly have the full story from the child anyway.'

Ailish seems somewhat triumphant now, so when Charlie continues his silence, the tone of voice from the other end of the phone moves up a gear.

'I knew it! Your poor wife may have been blind but I'm not, I knew there was something going on. Vera often talked about her never being sure of what was going on in your head at times, and lately I knew what she meant. I could see the faraway look in your eyes and the distracted furrowed brow. It was like you were there but not there. But never did I suspect what you were thinking about doing. Mother of God, 'twas madness. Surely even you know that now. And the incredible part of all is that you foretold it a full year earlier in that play. Any man who can write a play about something he is thinking of doing, and actually puts it on stage before he does it in real life, ought to have his head examined. I remember Vera being very upset last year when she read that play, but as ever you talked her out of it. I'll give you one thing, Charlie, you were good at that.'

Charlie suddenly finds fight from somewhere.

'I don't remember you being interested in anything I wrote.'

'I am now, Charlie, I am now.'

And with that the phone goes dead.

The conversation, and its abrupt ending, upsets Charlie more than he realises and for more than the obvious reason. Ailish and he had always got on really well since he'd met Vera over twelve years previously. While Vera was serious, Ailish was lighter and the three of them often went out together. At times, rightly or wrongly, Charlie often felt that Vera wasn't exactly happy whenever that happened and seemed to struggle with the ease between Charlie and Ailish which seemed at times to escape Charlie and her.

He held a deep respect for Ailish and felt it was mutual. So her anger at him right now troubles him deeply as the rest of the day drags on.

It occurs to him that while Marianne had taken great care in ensuring that the child was safe over here, his own focus had been on trying to keep her happy. And he's now fully aware of how much they've both risked to have the three of them under the one roof. Now it seems that their massive gamble has failed, not in a manner of a horse that comes second, but rather that of a horse that has had to be put down.

To give his head a rest, he lies on the couch for a while and recalls how Marianne and he had first met while he was still only a fledgling young man committed to religious life, while she was someone who had contemplated such a life at one stage but had quickly changed her mind. To share precious forbidden time with her back then, he had been willing to take risks with his life direction, just like now.

And if the universe at the time had decreed that they be cruelly cut adrift from each other, it seemed the same universe that had decreed they find each other again a little over a year earlier. A magnetically appealing young girl had flourished into an equally magnetically appealing woman. Charlie had found her energetic get-up-and-go to be in pleasant contrast to his indecisiveness, both as a young man and today.

Now, aged thirty-three, five foot six inches tall and of slim build, Marianne could command the attention of any room. Her green eyes and long wavy brown hair hung below her shoulders, her dazzling smile and porcelain skin capable of captivating any audience in seconds. She was funny, but with a serious side, smart without ever showing it off.

He reflected on how, a little over four weeks previously, the miracle had happened when she had picked him and his daughter up at Luton Airport.

And when they had stopped for food on their way home, Marianne just seemed to know exactly how to make the child feel at ease and loved, as they selected Mary Elizabeth's favourite meal together.

When they arrived at her home in 125 West St, now to be their new home, Mary Elizabeth couldn't get over that the room had been specially prepared for her, decorated perfectly for a girl her age, with several stuffed toys on her pillow. Charlie's dreamworld had materialised and it felt like absolute perfection. If only the world could have stood still in that moment. But it never does, and it didn't.

...the cold hard facts of life...

When Charlie awoke abruptly from a restless night and saw his beloved little girl alongside him in a strange bed, in what was for her a strange house, and in a strange country, the cold shiver of reality ran down his spine.

His daughter's marvel at her room turned to unease when he said that Marianne didn't have children, leading to the child's next question highlighting the house-of-cards nature of this shaky paradise.

'Then why has she done up the room specially for me, when we're only staying a few days?'

His lie of last week about the nature and length of their stay had already been found out.

And, to further complicate an already complicated situation, try as he might, Charlie could not shut out the visceral picture of a crying Vera in what was up to yesterday his home of eleven years, and hearing her voice piercing his unslept brain, 'What in the name of God have you done, Charlie?'

And he asked himself the same question.

Charlie's first real morning in Dunstable would get much more real. If he had hoped that Marianne might have organised a type of tourist integration day to Dunstable for the child, he was mistaken. Being more of a pragmatist than Charlie, Marianne had made different plans entirely. A series of appointments had been made, firstly with the local Catholic Primary School in Dunstable, quickly followed by one with a solicitor.

The child found it weird that she would have to go to school during a 'little holiday', but by now Charlie was good at explaining things which were not easy to explain. It was all just a piece of brief research, he explained, for her to experience primary education in a school in a different education system and with children of different cultures.

And because she loved and trusted her father, the innocent child seemed ok with that.

The second appointment was a much tougher assignment for Charlie, with a solicitor to initiate ward-of-court proceedings regarding Mary Elizabeth.

If his easily-accessed guilt had been steadily moving from an observation post to a worried stance since his arrival here, it felt like someone had set fire to it in that solicitor's office when he heard the legal reality of what he had done, to such a degree that he walked out, with the task incomplete.

After that, the reality of the separate and together lives of all three stakeholders in this romantically but possibly foolishly conceived utopia became more visible with each passing hour. This was a million miles away from Charlie's one-day flying visit here only eight short weeks previously, but which now seemed like a lifetime ago.

They had hoped that Marianne's Uncle Robert would offer him work. But Robert seemed hesitant about what Marianne was taking on, and although eventually giving her permission to have Charlie and the child stay in 125 West St, he felt it better to hold the boundary around Charlie finding his own way in Dunstable. So, it had taken him two weeks to secure work in the field of insurance phone-sales. The relief at finding any job lifted his spirits and as he left his office each evening, he would remind himself that everything would in time fall into place.

But the longed-for falling into place never really happened, concluding with his difficult conversation with his daughter last night and the horrific events of earlier.

At that point, he knew he was wading far too deeply into dark and murky waters, so he decided to get up and walk to the local food store to grab a takeaway for both himself and Marianne. He had neither the heart, the appetite nor the energy to cook.

14

But, of course, the visit to the local store brought back a thousand memories of Mary Elizabeth's love of that shop that had so many different varieties of sweets, one of the few things over here which was better than home, she had concluded.

He put the takeaways in the oven as he tried to predict the many twists and turns the conversation with Marianne might take. There was one thing for sure. She would need reassurances that the events of this morning would not alter their plans to be together. And right now, in his broken state, he didn't feel he could offer her that reassurance.

…it's where I wanna be…

It was a May late afternoon after school in 1966 as thirteen-year-old Marianne McAndrew found herself anxiously standing outside the convent door, having pressed the brass doorbell. She was here to see Sister Teresa on a very important matter. Marianne was considered tall for her age, slim, with long light-brown hair falling to her shoulders.

One of the more unusual features of the town in which she and her mother lived was the fact that it contained two religious communities, a convent and a monastery. Such communities were common enough in the Ireland of the '60's and '70s, but to have two in the one town was a bit special, she thought.

She had recently been to a cinema as part of a school trip to see the recently-released film *The Sound of Music* and had been very taken with the character of the young nun. And typical of her impetuosity, here she stood, nervously waiting outside at the large imposing oak convent door, looking up and around at the grey limestone building.

She felt so relieved when it was Sister Teresa who answered, her favourite teacher in sixth class, that she immediately broke into tears.

'Good Lord, Marianne, come in.'

Marianne did so and slowly took in the array of holy pictures and dark mahogany furniture everywhere, including a huge staircase, in the vast entrance hall of the convent. It was just like she had seen in the film, comforting but imposing.

When Marianne was seated in one of the two armchairs, in what appeared to the child as being a visitor's room, with a large table, six chairs and two armchairs, Sister Teresa gently queried, 'Now Marianne, what's with all the tears?'

'I want to be a nun, just like you,' she anxiously blurted out in case she might either forget it or lose courage.

'And the thought of being a nun makes you cry? It's not that bad, you know.'

At that, Marianne lost her frown as her pretty face broke into a smile.

'I didn't mean that.'

'Thank God for that.' Sister Teresa smiled. 'Now, can you say a bit more about wanting to become a nun?'

Marianne, in fear of rejection, replied, 'When someone asks me to say more about an idea I have, it usually means they don't think that it's a good idea in the first place.'

'And why would I not think that it's a good idea?'

'Because everyone thinks I'm too impulsive for my own good, that this notion of wanting to become a nun will pass in a few weeks, and that I'll change my mind and get excited about something else altogether,' she replied. 'But I won't, I know I won't.'

Sister Teresa held up a hand as if to slow Marianne down.

'You do know that I'm relatively new to this convent, so perhaps you'd tell me a little bit about yourself, apart from what I already know of you from class, which is that you're a good-humoured young lady and an attentive student who tries hard.'

'What would you like to know?'

'Marianne is a beautiful name. Did your mam choose that name, it being somewhat like Maria?'

'No, my dad picked it. He loved Marianne Faithful and was forever playing her songs on his old record player.'

On mentioning her dad, Marianne's voice trembled as a big tear fell from one of her eyes, which didn't go unnoticed by Sister Teresa.

'You mention your dad in the past tense.'

'He went to heaven three years ago.'

This was followed by more tears, at which point Sister Teresa put her arms around her young guest.

17

'Tell you what, Marianne, why don't we have this conversation with your mam present. I think that would be better all round, don't you?'

Young and enthusiastic Marianne wasn't at all sure that was such a good idea.

'You tell her about my wanting to become a nun, and that will end that,' she said forlornly.

'No, I promise I will not. But I guess I'm kind of hoping you might tell her yourself when you're both here.'

Marianne reluctantly agreed to a meeting between all three, arranged for the following Saturday morning, which Marianne thought seemed ages away. But it wasn't.

And when Marianne and her mother arrived back as agreed at the convent on the following Saturday morning, Sister Teresa greeted them by saying she would like to talk to the mam, Maria, on her own for a while if that was ok, but assured Marianne that, in that conversation, she would not be sharing anything that had been told her in confidence.

Looking at Maria, Sister Teresa could see where Marianne at least partially got her good looks from, including her height. Whilst her face was undoubtedly showing some signs of a hard life, her natural facial beauty still shone through and she would be considered to be a very attractive thirty-two-year-old woman, Sister Teresa thought, with her dark brown hair neatly tied up. Her dress sense was quite artistic, which may have been influenced by her job at her sister's art & craft shop.

And, as Maria took in the good nun, her first thoughts were *she's like a nun*, but on further reflection, could see that she was of medium height with a full figure, had a kind face and demeanour, and seemed to be a happy and contented person. She seemed somewhere around her own age with a look of contentment about her, which Maria thought might have come from either an easy life or her being so close to God.

With Marianne feeling reassured and given tea and biscuits in a different room, her mam Maria proceeded to give some relevant family background to the attentive nun.

Marianne's dad's family, the McAndrews, were a well-to-do family and had held lofty ambitions for their two sons, of which Marianne's father Paul was the youngest. The older brother, Robert, had been awarded a First Class Master's Degree in Engineering and had moved to Dunstable in England, where he worked with one of the big construction companies, before eventually taking over that company five years previously. Paul, equally bright, was apparently destined for similar academic and business success. But at age eighteen, he fell in love with a local girl.

Here, Maria's account of the story became very emotional.

'That girl was me. And, to put it mildly, I certainly didn't measure up to the ideal daughter-in-law vision of either his parents.'

Maria went on to explain that, to make matters worse, such mutual love can lead to an unplanned pregnancy. And that is precisely what happened. Paul was immediately informed that financial arrangements would be put in place to make sure that Maria wouldn't want for anything, whether that meant she would take the boat to England or raise the child on her own. Hence their shock when Paul told them with a great degree of certainty that he was honouring his commitment to Maria and the unborn child, and that he looked forward to marrying her. She recalled him holding her hand as he proudly told his parents that he had acquired an apprenticeship with a local carpenter, which was met with a combination of scorn and ridicule, while his mother pleaded with him to have the wedding somewhere away from here.

But Paul had stood by his word. As a result, neither of his parents attended what was a very quiet wedding in Maria's local church. But Robert, showing a spirit of decency, returned from Dunstable for the occasion. Six months later, Marianne was born, and the new McAndrew family set up home in a cottage which had been home to her mother, prior to her recent long-term placement in residential care. And, despite what Paul's parents might term 'their irregular family foundation,' Maria, Paul and baby Marianne were very happy there.

Then disaster struck. Paul fell off a roof at work when Marianne was only six years old, resulting in him being confined to a wheelchair. Of course, his boss was not adequately insured, so money inevitably became an issue, leading to Maria taking up part-time work in the town's art shop, owned by her sister, Julie.

Life had carried on that way till one day when the poor child, unexpectedly home from school early as her teacher was sick, couldn't find her father in the house. After calling and calling his name in a blind panic, she ran outside to the shed and found him unresponsive in his wheelchair. It seemed that he had been making a small wheelbarrow for her as she had requested, to enable her to help with bringing in firewood. He had suffered a massive coronary and died three days later in hospital without ever regaining consciousness. Marianne was only ten years old.

Sister Teresa allowed a respectful silence to show proper respect to Maria's story before speaking.

'That makes sense, then.'

'Makes sense?'

'I'll let her tell you all about that herself,' Sister Teresa concluded, before calling Marianne back into the room.

The wise nun decided to change the subject completely as she addressed them both.

'I thought the beautiful name Marianne had been chosen after your mother, but apparently not so.'

'That's right,' Maria replied. 'She's named after her dad's secret crush, Marianne Faithful.'

20

Marianne seemed to find that funny at first but then began to cry.

When the two adults had gently comforted her, it was agreed that Marianne would be offered grief support, which would be set up by Sister Teresa. This seemed to please the teenager.

'Now, Marianne, don't you have something else to share with your mam?' Sister Teresa asked.

Marianne was silent for a while, caught in a space between the sad memories around her dad and the reason she had come to see Sister Teresa during the week.

She slowly caught her mother's eye and gravely announced, 'I want to be a nun.'

Her mam seemed genuinely taken aback.

'That's a big step, pet,' Maria said, just as Sister Teresa had predicted.

But, as Sister Teresa had promised her, Marianne's idea of a vocation was listened to, with genuine praise from both. After much discussion, all three agreed that, while Marianne's plans to become a nun someday were noble and genuine, perhaps she would think about it for a while.

So an agreement was drawn up that Marianne would take up the offer of grief support by Sister Teresa and, at an agreed date in the future, they would meet again about her possible vocational aspirations.

Marianne's grief meetings began on the following week, and over the following weeks and months, she found it helped her to come to terms with her sad young life to date, especially her father's tragic passing and the way his family had disowned him. At age thirteen, Marianne had learned quite a lot about life and the difference between good and bad.

She often reflected in later years that, without this crucial support, she could and probably would have grown into a very angry and bitter young woman.

This awareness included that, as time moved on, she found that she was increasingly liking the company of young men, so when the time came around for the review of her fledging vocation, she acknowledged to her mother and Sister Teresa that she now wanted to research her liking of boys for another while. It seemed Marianne McAndrew had decided there might be more to life than joining a convent.

...we're caught in a trap...

Back in 125 West St, at last Charlie saw Marianne's bus pull up. He quickly transferred the food from the oven to the pre-set table for two and looked out the window. As she stepped down from the bus, he could see that, even in her office clothes, she was a striking-looking woman and he longed to feel what he had felt when she had stepped from the bus outside that garden centre not so terribly long ago. But now, with his heart divided, such feelings refused to engage.

As she walked up the small garden path between the street and the front door, he thought she looked troubled and vulnerable, but maybe that was just his imagination, for she could hardly know of this morning's events, or was it a projection of his own feelings onto her?

He stood at the front door and was greeted with her usual smile. Instinctively he knew that the events of that morning would ensure that such a warm smile would probably be a thing of the past, that nothing would ever be the same again, not for her, for him, or for them.

Marianne's face immediately changed when she noticed the table set for two.

'Where's Mary Elizabeth?' she asked.

'There's been a development,' Charlie said, looking at the ceiling.

'What kind of development?'

'Not a good one,' he said, still not able to look her in the eye.

'Tell me.' Marianne's look of concern was growing more noticeable by the second.

'Perhaps we should eat the food while it's hot.'

Charlie needed brief respite, but Marianne clearly didn't.

'As if I could. Please, Charlie, where is Mary Elizabeth?'

'She's gone,' was all he could come up with.

'Gone?' she asked incredulously.

Charlie resorted to the refuge of the white lie, or as he preferred to call it, a strategic approach.

'She wasn't very happy here, so her aunt came for her earlier today. She's on her way back home.'

'Without telling me?'

Once the lie floodgate had been opened, it seemed easier for Charlie to keep going in that direction.

'I thought it best.'

But he wasn't getting off that lightly.

'Best for whom?'

'For all of us.'

'Did you not think of speaking to me about such a decision?'

He hesitated.

'Charlie, please look me straight in the eye. Something's happened and it's not what you say has happened, so please don't patronise me by telling me to eat.'

Tears now appeared in Charlie's eyes.

'Tell me, Charlie, for God's sake, just tell me!'

The urgency in her voice broke Charlie.

'She was taken as I walked her to school.'

'Taken?'

'Snatched, abducted, kidnapped, take your pick,' he replied bluntly, letting the morning's stress show.

'Snatched? By whom?'

'By someone who felt she belonged back home, I presume.'

Marianne was stunned

'Oh my God! How can you be so sure?'

Charlie was drowning now.

'I've been speaking to her aunt, her mother's sister, Ailish.'

Marianne's eyes turned to heaven in disbelief.

'Before you spoke to me?'

Charlie could only reply, 'I'm sorry, but I had to know she was safe.'

Marianne sighed.

'So she's been snatched. I thought this could happen.'

'I know you did.'

'Did you call the police?'

'Call them? I've given half the bloody morning down at the police station.' His quickly diminishing window of tolerance leading to his being snappy with her was followed quickly by, 'I'm sorry.'

At this, Marianne softened and put her arms around him.

'Are they searching for her?'

Charlie confirmed that they were but had not reported back to him as yet.

The fuller picture of this morning was now taking shape for Marianne.

'The bus had to take a detour this morning and I wondered why.' Marianne reached across the table and took Charlie's two hands in hers. 'Forgive me, I'm just in shock. You're right. Let's eat and then you can tell me everything.'

As they both tried to eat something they had no mind for, Charlie slowly began to share the sad narrative with her of all that had happened since she had left the house that morning for work, ending again with, 'I'm so sorry.'

'And that was why I wanted to make her a ward of court, the day after ye both arrived here.'

'I know,' was all Charlie could muster in reply.

'I know how upset you are now, but I need to know why you didn't go through with it, Charlie. The police would be in a much stronger position now if that had been secured. They'd be keeping watch at every airport and sea-ferry terminal. We would get her back.'

'They're searching anyhow. They told me that.'

Marianne persisted in making her point. 'But without the ward of court papers their hands are tied. Do you not see that?'

Charlie had had a rough day, and in that moment and his tired state, he wasn't at all sure that he had done the wrong thing in walking out of that solicitor's office.

'That solicitor treated me like some kind of imbecile,' he said defensively as he attempted to imitate the solicitor's English accent. '*You do realise, I hope, what you have done is extremely serious.* Of course I fucking knew!'

'I know,' Marianne said softly. 'He pretty much said the same to me when I made the appointment. I'd impressed upon him that it was essential the child needed to be with you for her safety. So he had explained that all that was necessary was for you to swear an affidavit to that effect before him and a clerk of the court.'

Charlie fully realised at this stage that he would be much better to leave this conversation for another time, but he ploughed on in his tiredness, regardless of the fall.

'What did you mean by *to that effect*?'

'To the effect that you believed the child was in danger at home.'

This met with the anger of a conflicted Charlie.

'You absolutely had no right to tell him that.'

'But you had told me that Mary Elizabeth's safety was at stake.'

Now Charlie's divided loyalties showed themselves in all their true colours.

'I may have said something like that at one point, but the situation had changed.'

'But you said…' she began to protest but was swiftly stopped in her tracks.

'Well, whatever the hell I might or might not have said, it was meant to be a private conversation between you and me, not to be spread all over the bloody place over here.'

Marianne wouldn't let it go.

'But Charlie, do you not understand? Even if the events of this morning had not occurred, we wouldn't have been legally able to keep her here anyhow without her being

26

made a ward of court at some point. You know that her school have been asking for updates on that situation.'

'I know,' Charlie conceded, 'but in that solicitor's office, I suddenly choked between us wanting her here with us and it being absolutely crucial to the child's safety.'

Marianne's response was gentle. 'Can you please help me to understand why?'

'The child's mother Vera would have enough to deal with by my taking her only child, without her being accused of neglecting the child.'

'So you couldn't upset Vera?' Marianne asked incredulously.

'I could and I did,' he replied, 'but I couldn't be unfair to her.'

'And you don't think what you did to her in actually bringing the child over here four weeks ago was unfair?'

Charlie went silent.

With that, Marianne lowered her head and asked, 'Did you ask the aunt if she knew who organised such a despicable act?'

He shook his head.

'Are you going to ask her?'

Charlie's response was almost inaudible. 'Probably not.'

Marianne had seemingly heard enough.

'I don't like what I think you are feeling right now, and I certainly don't like what I'm feeling. I'm going to bed, Charlie. I think its best if you sleep in the child's room for now while we both reflect on where this development actually leaves us.'

She immediately took herself upstairs, leaving Charlie feeling alone in a way he'd rarely previously felt. He cleaned up the dishes almost unconsciously, like a learned coping skill from when he felt he was in trouble, before in turn making his own way up the stairs. But one look inside Mary Elizabeth's room was more than he could bear.

So he grabbed a blanket from a press and settled himself on the couch in the living room, the same couch from which he and Marianne had lovingly watched *Ryan's Daughter* in a romantic and much simpler setting. Ironically, it was a film about an affair that goes horribly wrong. Without consciously knowing it, Marianne and Charlie had acted out the theme of that film to within an inch of its life.

...this morning I'm just leaving, but come sunset I'll be gone...

It was approaching midday on September 1st, 1965.

Charlie's thirteenth birthday had been only a few short weeks previously, as he found himself sitting in the small kitchen, staring out the open small back window of this farmer's cottage home at nothing in particular, a vacant reflective stare rather than a purposeful stare. But if his stare wasn't focussed, his mind was. The window he would be staring out of the next day would be different, much bigger, and would be looking onto an entirely different world, far away from his home and family, and far away from his beloved mother, Maggie.

Charlie liked his quaint home with its small windows, galvanised roof, small front door and porch. There was no hallway or back door. In the absence of a hall, each room to the right of the porch led to the next, and so to get to the end room, you had to walk through the others.

This was apart from the one room to the left of the porch, interestingly called the 'good room', the only room which was kept locked. This room was preserved for important documents and important visitors, like the parish priest, the doctor or the schoolmaster etc. As far as Charlie and his siblings were concerned, this room was strictly out of bounds.

When Bro Marcus came to visit their home sometime after Charlie's parents' application on his behalf for acceptance to an Order of Brothers, that room was the venue where relevant paperwork was read and signed by Bro Marcus and in turn signed by Charlie and his parents.

He remembered thinking how tall Bro Marcus was compared to his father who was small and wiry. Because Charlie was tall for his age, there was a quiet standing private joke between Charlie and his only sibling, his brother Marty who was six years older than him, about their next-door neighbour being a tall man.

Charlie's awareness around that simple doorstep being the divide between everyday life and a completely different world, was perhaps a suitable metaphor between where he was right now and where he would be in a few hours time, stepping from his childhood to a grown-up world, from being carefree to very much having to be full of care.

Because of the low door and small windows at home, the house generally seemed somewhat dark, but it was homely and cosy. He suspected that the house he was going to would not be so homely or cosy. It would be bigger, with bigger windows and doors, with higher ceilings and statues, but he wasn't quite so sure about the cosiness. This cosiness at home was largely due to the big open fire always alight in the winter. Fuelled by logs Marty and his father would cut, and an old-fashioned fuel called culm-balls. These consisted of coal dust, derived at the time from an old nearby disused coal mine, mixed with yellow clay as a binding agent and moulded into small, compressed balls. This was quite a specialist job, only carried out by Charlie's father, Martin.

His mother christened their home *The Little Tin House*, reflecting her simplicity, humility and strong faith, the latter not always shared as enthusiastically by his father.

Charlie's thoughts were interrupted by his mother coming from her room and placing an old and faded suitcase on the table in front of him. Maggie was a good-looking woman, even if her figure now was more reflective of her giving birth to two boys and her outdoor work on the farm. She used to joke that the neighbours didn't know she was pregnant either time till she was seen walking up the road with a pram. She was taller than her husband, fresh-faced with dark brown hair. She mostly wore a pinafore in the house which was replaced with an outdoors coat and a woolly hat which she christened 'the thing for my head' when going outside to help on the farm, which was quite often.

'I was hoping to get you a new case, Charlie,' she said, 'but you know how hard it is to get to town to get anything like that.'

'It will do grand, Mam.'

Young Charlie understood completely. Everyone had their specific chores on the small farm on which his father worked his own fingers to the bone, while Marty also played his part in the farm chores, despite having a full-time job. Charlie's main chores were going to the local village for messages for his mother and to whichever neighbour might be going through a hard time, with home-grown potatoes and vegetables. And Maggie was not excluded from the outdoor chores, specialising in the area of the more delicate farming tasks, such as feeding new-born calves. There was little time for going to town or any other such luxuries for anyone.

Besides, Charlie would have said or done anything to make life easier for his mother. For he knew her life not to be easy, but admired that she always seemed to be content with her lot in life. Her love for and loyalty to his father and her two boys put her in sainthood territory in his opinion. She led a simple life with little desire to go outside her home, except to Mass and to get groceries from the village on her bike.

'I think I have everything you will need in there,' Maggie said softly as she handed him the suitcase.

Like Charlie, she too had been very quiet all morning since Charlie's father and their neighbour Digger Maguire had gone to cover in a grave of a neighbour buried earlier that morning.

'I'm sure it's perfect, Mam.'

'How I wish, Charlie, how I wish.'

She noticed that the home-baked brown bread on the table had not been touched, as was the case with the homemade jam.

'You haven't eaten?'

'I'm not hungry.'

A mother's protective instincts immediately kicked in.

'You know you don't have to go, there's still time.'

'My father thinks that it's the right place for me.'

But Maggie wanted her youngest son to know there was still time for a change of mind.

'If you have any doubts at all, I can get around your father.'

But Charlie was resigned. He had been for the past few weeks.

'No, everything's ready. I'll be grand when I get there.'

'I wish they'd hurry up,' was her anxious reply before she hastily took herself into the next room, where he could hear her cry.

'I'm going for a stroll, but won't be long,' he said as he went outside, partly to give her space to cry and partly to give himself the same option.

Charlie stood alone in the shed, remembering his younger self as a sad and scared young fella and how this old cow shed acted as a place of refuge, a place where he felt entirely safe, so it was a good place for him to wonder why in fact he had made the decision a few months previously to enter a monastery.

One reason was that neither Martin nor himself believed that he could ever make a farmer. Any help Martin might need would be better served by Digger and Marty. Another was that Martin, whilst a good hard-working man, didn't have much faith in formal education. Neither did he believe in the expense of a car, and school buses did not as yet feature on the Irish landscape. So the default education pathway for young men like Charlie was the Group

Certificate at the local Tech, a course that didn't excite Charlie very much.

Marty had gone that route and was now happily working with a local builder. And even though Marty thought Charlie was stone mad to be thinking of going to a monastery, he could see that Charlie was different to him. Neither expected the other to fully understand.

Charlie had found the outside world to be an unfair and uncaring place. He was aware that his village consisted of a few sensitive people and a lot of insensitive ones, and that life would be perhaps always a struggle for the sensitive ones and equally realised that his village acted somewhat as a vignette to the world in that regard.

Looking around the shed, from one of the higher shelves from the shelf unit Marty had made as part of his Group Cert training, his eye caught an old one-page programme from a show he'd had the rare privilege of attending a few winters previously. It was of a comedy called *Charlie's Aunt*, performed in the local village hall with its elevated stage, where on occasion a visiting group of players would perform. That particular privilege came compliment of his very own "Charlie's Aunt", his beloved Aunt Maureen, sister of his mother, who had bought sweets for the two of them in the nearby shop beforehand.

Maureen, as was quietly referred to at the time, "wasn't well", which was sometimes reflected in her being overweight, her general demeanour and sometimes in her facial expressions and sense of dress, which was inevitably out of sync with the weather, the seasons and most certainly with the fashion of the day.

But Charlie didn't care much for that kind of talk about his aunt or in fact about any human being. He loved her. And, in the rather serious environment of small farm endless tasks, it was she who had introduced him to a less serious world of surrealism, comics, drama, music, fun, going on the bus to the nearest town for gadgets like watches, cameras and torches. Without knowing it, she had also introduced him to the world of difference and people's choice of understanding or being ignorant about that word.

Sadly for Charlie, on this the most important day of his young life, Maureen was in the nearest psychiatric hospital on one of many long-stay visits there. If she had been well, Charlie would have a span-new suitcase, the best that money could buy. There would be nothing surer.

Such nostalgic and philosophical thoughts were halted by the sound of Digger's car pulling into the yard and his mother calling out to him.

'They're here, Charlie.'

Charlie saw his father going into the other outhouse as his mother ushered Digger into the kitchen. Martin McCann was a hardy wiry farmer, only about five foot six inches with a thin build which belied his strength and ability to suffer the kind of hardship that a small, scattered farm can bring.

Digger was a hard man to describe. There wasn't anything outstanding about him, but he had all the appearance of a hardworking man, permanently dressed in overalls, a pair of green wellington boots and a woolly hat over a permanent weatherbeaten ruddy complexion.

The young man decided to join his mother and Digger in the kitchen, but as he approached, he realised they were talking about him so he decided to go out of sight and to eavesdrop from the rear window.

'Martin is gone looking at that Friesian cow, Maggie. Is the young fella ready?'

'He'll be ready in a minute, Digger. Tis good of you to bring him on this long journey.'

'It's what neighbours do, Maggie. When I have problems with a cow calving, Martin McCann's the man I'll call, and when ye need a lift anywhere, Digger Maguire's the man ye'll call. It works both ways, Maggie.'

'If you say so, Digger, if you say so.' Maggie smiled.

'How's that young fella about going where he's going?' Digger enquired in his own inimitable way of asking.

Maggie paused for a long time before answering.

'He seemed ok all along, but this morning I think he's not so sure about it. He's gone very quiet. I wonder if we're doing the right thing at all, Digger. Maybe I could have said something sooner. I mean, it can hardly be right to bring young boys of thirteen into religious life before they've seen anything of the world, can it?'

'Maybe,' Digger replied, 'but sure, let him off and see how he gets on. You know, Maggie, if he's not happy there, Digger Maguire will be up that road for him like I was in the local mountain rally.'

At this point, Charlie saw his father coming out of the outhouse and heading for the kitchen, so he followed quietly, saying, 'I'm ready,' as he entered the house.

'Your father's changing his clothes, he won't be a minute,' Maggie replied.

Charlie looked at his mother in surprise. 'Are you not coming?'

'No, Charlie,' she said softly. 'Your father thinks it's best that I don't.'

And so Charlie headed off to Chapel Hill House in the back of Digger's Ford Anglia. Digger lived alone, so the back seat of his car was more used for transporting dogs or even small calves than humans, but Charlie was too preoccupied with where he was going to even notice. What he did notice as they were pulling out of the yard was a picture that broke his young heart. As he turned to look out the back window, he saw his mother crying at the front door, an image that upset him desperately. Being so preoccupied by all that he would miss, he hadn't fully thought out how much his mother would miss him, the only man in the house she could really talk to, and for all the little jobs he used do for her, unnoticed by the others.

Chapel Hill was only fifty odd miles from his home, but for a young boy coming from a home that had no car, it seemed like he was being transported to a different planet. As the journey progressed, Digger and his father were chatting away about things, things that were important to them, like the Friesian cow that was about to calf, how a bull calf would be much more valuable than a heifer and about the big turnout at Jackie Daly's funeral.

As Charlie sat looking out at the countryside, which was getting stranger by the mile, he wanted to tell them to turn around, that he had made a mistake, but how could he, especially when he heard his father telling Digger how lucky young Charlie was to be getting into a grand place like Chapel Hill for the Winter.

And after what seemed like the longest yet shortest journey of his young life, they finally drove up the avenue to the daunting-looking grey building, with white window frames and a large wood door, painted black, which was to be his home for the next six years, Chapel Hill House of Prayer.

…can't hide and I just can't fake it…

Back in Dunstable, Charlie had woken early from his couch on yet another Friday morning, three long and lonely weeks since his daughter's abduction, just as he had done every morning since he'd been asked to sleep there.

His sister-in-law Ailish had confirmed a few days after the abduction that Mary Elizabeth had gotten safely back to Ireland. And, as promised, Charlie had passed on this information to the police, genuinely not knowing, or appearing to want to know, who might have been behind it all. The police had contacted the Garda station in Charlie's home village who confirmed the child was safely home and seemingly happy there.

The Gardai did ask a few questions of the child's mother and her sister, but as far as anyone was concerned, the child had simply arrived safely back home after visiting her father in England, was happy to be home as were all those who loved her, and no one was willing to say or even speculate as to how that event might have happened.

The Bedfordshire Police were continuing their investigations into the assault, but felt, without Charlie's co-operation, there wasn't much more for them to do, so the legal end of things was pretty much wrapped up at that.

Not so in 125 West St, where a stalemate had descended, like a heavy fog refusing to lift. Marianne and Charlie had agreed they would talk that night to decide if they would either move ahead as a couple or as nothing at all.

As he reflected on his sister-in-law's reference to his need to have his head examined, Charlie began to wonder if in fact there might be some truth in that.

He was struggling with the contradictory split within him that had become so much more obvious to him since his arrival in Dunstable. Having felt so strongly for such a long time that he and Marianne were perfect together, to a point where every day without her brought such heartache, now in a similar but contradictory manner, every day they were together seemed to bring the same heartache that being apart once did. For, in this new situation, his being with Marianne meant his being kept apart from his daughter, and Charlie's primal longing to be with his daughter was increasingly growing to the obvious detriment of the other. He knew it and Marianne knew it.

But he equally instinctively knew that, if his actions in coming here had proven to be one big mistake, leaving here could constitute an even bigger one. So, for the past three weeks, he had honestly tried to do the right thing in giving himself sufficient space to make a proper decision, whatever that might be, recognising all the stakeholders involved. But he was finding that time was not providing the answer he so desperately sought.

In fairness, Marianne had tried to keep the situation as normal as possible, including discreetly putting the radio on when she got home from work as she had always done since his arrival. If the chief purpose of this was to maintain some semblance of normality, it also served to drown out the overwhelming gulf of silence that had developed between them. But, like everything she tried, it too proved to be a counterproductive move. Madonna's "La Isla Bonita" seemed to be constantly on the radio at the time, a lively catchy song, the lyrics of which – *A young girl with eyes like the desert. It all seems like yesterday, not far away* – got to Charlie to the point of his going out into the small unkept garden at the rear of the house.

A week earlier, he had received a distressing letter from his mother, stating that he would be welcome to return back home, but that he should do so now. *Mary Elizabeth seems very happy to be home but is constantly asking when her daddy is coming*, the letter stated, and adding as Maggie would, *We still love you, Charlie, but the child needs to know what's happening one way or the other*. Her letter also included that, if he made that decision, he'd be welcome to stay with them, but if that proved awkward as they lived alongside Vera's home, his brother Marty, now aged forty and living alone only a mile away since his recent separation, had said he could live there in the short term.

He had not shared this letter with Marianne, and he knew why. He found himself in no-man's land, being physically unavailable to his daughter and emotionally unavailable to Marianne.

But as he struggled to get off the couch that morning, it dawned on him that no such comfort blanket as the *proper* decision would ever present itself. It would have to be *his* decision, with a seemingly huge price to be paid whatever he decided.

To make matters worse, his initial success as an insurance salesman had suddenly nosedived along with everything else. He wasn't bringing money in, his mind wasn't focussed and he wasn't sleeping properly.

He still felt the old familiar paralysis around difficult decisions and was secretly hoping that Marianne would make the decision for him, just as the unexpected events three weeks earlier had relieved him of that other difficult dilemma. He felt sorry for Marianne, but in light of their new circumstances, he knew he couldn't please everyone.

But there was the other question. What would *home* be like now? His mother's letter hadn't spared him the reality of what he'd have to face. What he had done was the talk of the parish, and photographs of him and Mary Elizabeth from that drama festival final from the previous year had been published in some of what she called rag Sunday papers under the heading "Tug of Love child safely back home."

Would Vera allow him back in his former home ever again, and if so, under what conditions? And if he couldn't be under the same roof as his child, was there much difference between being there and here? He spent most of the day in that type of grief-stricken maze with no apparent way out.

By the time Marianne got home from work later that evening, nothing had shifted in Charlie's brain as they silently ate and sat down to talk as agreed. Marianne had equally been thinking and had obviously decided that small talk would be of little help,

'You're not happy,' she began.

Charlie didn't answer but his body language told its own story.

'I'm sad for you,' she said, 'but I'm equally angry with you.'

'I know,' was all he could say before she continued.

'I still can't get my head around why you refused to swear whatever it was you were required to swear, to make sure Mary Elizabeth could have remained here, at least till the court hearing.'

'I didn't want any bloody court hearing!'

If Marianne was shocked, so was Charlie. He knew what he had been thinking, but never meant to say it out loud. But what's said cannot be unsaid and he now felt that their decision had probably been made in that outburst.

Marianne eventually broke the silence calmly.

'Let me get this much straight. You thought you could bring your child over here without her mother's consent and that she'd be allowed to remain here without presenting any just reason for doing so.'

'Something like that,' Charlie muttered.

'I believe at this point, Charlie, that not alone is your heart back in Ireland, but so is your head.'

'I don't know,' said Charlie, beginning to sound like a broken record at this point.

'Tell me, Charlie, what exactly is it that you want? It seems that, while you're very definitely missing Mary Elizabeth, you have made absolutely no attempt to get her back, and that makes me extremely nervous. That kind of silent mind game can lead a woman to dark places.'

'Maybe we can still work this out,' he said unconvincingly.

'How?'

'I don't know.'

'Is that what you want?'

'I don't know.'

'And is that what you believe I want?'

'I hope so,' he said as he began to cry.

Marianne looked at his childlike lost and broken face.

She took him by the hand and silently led him upstairs.

…love is now the reason I must go…

It was the morning after the night before, as Marianne awoke early and heard Charlie move beside her. It was nice to have him back in her bed, she thought as she quietly rose and went about getting ready for work. Taking him to her bed last night was perhaps her last loving attempt to shift something in him. But in honesty, she herself needed the comfort of his closeness.

She awoke him with a coffee and toast and told him that if he needed to return to be with his child, she would understand, but that she wouldn't see any point in their continuing communication. It would simply be too hard on both of them. After all, they had given it their best shot, and perhaps it was from the beginning a long shot.

They would both have to accept that fact. He had looked rather shocked, but did say that he could understand. She kissed him before leaving, but his response didn't seem to be fully reciprocative.

So she decided to walk to work to give herself space to reflect on all that had been said and done the previous evening. She could feel the summer heat as she walked and felt it was a shame to be in such a crisis in this beautiful weather, as she could see people preparing to head out for picnics and lawnmowers being started up in lots of gardens. Whatever the outcome of last night would be, this gorgeous summer morning seemed to be perhaps a pretty good place to start.

But her mind wouldn't settle in work at all that morning, seeing such sadness in Charlie's face as she left and realising that he wasn't the only one feeling sad. On the one hand, her love for him was regretting the black and white proposition she had put to him, but on the other, her love for herself was assuring her that he simply could not have the best of both worlds. In fairness to him, she thought, he had

42

tried to make this work, but perhaps such plans are simply not always meant to be.

Not having a child herself, she could only guess at what he must be feeling or about the divisive situation he found himself in.

Her strong sense of conflict and unease continued all through that morning and into the afternoon, to the point that she decided to leave work early.

The moment she stepped off the bus, and saw the front curtains closed, her heart closed in on itself to the point of passing out.

When she finally got the key in the door, she saw the letter left on the kitchen table.

26th May 1986

Marianne,

I find myself in an impossible situation. I know you will say, with some degree of fairness, that I have created this situation for myself, with my naivety and stubbornness.

Either way, this impossible situation means that I find my heart torn asunder between my love of Mary Elizabeth and my love for you. I thought I could have you both, but that dream has now been irrevocably shattered.

Which means I must choose.

They are two such completely different loves that I find it impossible to compare, to explain, other than to call on the genius of John Denver's lyrics, "Love is why I came here in the first place. Love is now the reason I must go." So, I am allowing my actions to reflect my conflicted decision rather than words.

I know that, since Mary Elizabeth was taken, I have disappointed you and let you down, and now I am doing so again, with even more cruelty. But, with my heart torn, it is equally cruel to stay, for I don't believe I will ever feel any differently than I do now. I can see that you've been so

*supportive and stoic about this whole sorry situation, but it
cannot continue.*

*You very definitely said yesterday that, if I choose to go,
there would be no point in us trying to remain in contact.*

I intend to respect that decision.
Charlie

Marianne sat there, numb, as she tried to process horrible
feelings of desertion, betrayal and grief as she immersed
herself in the full impact of the empty house. It was hard to
believe that a man so stuck in grief for three weeks could
suddenly become so proactive and leave her like this. Surely
she deserved better.

But, strangely, in this moment of sheer desolation,
Marianne's sympathy went to Mary Elizabeth's mother who
had also looked at an empty room and a letter from Charlie
on the same day as they arrived in 125 West St. In this
darkest of places, she knew with great certainty that she
would keep her word about no further contact. She knew
she could never go through all of this ever again, and neither
should the child's mother.

...I guess every form of refuge has its price...

As thirteen-year-old Charlie was taking in his first impressions of Chapel Hill, his father walked him to the heavily panelled front door and rang the bell. Bro James, a tall imposing-looking man, emerged from within. He was wearing a long black soutane with a sash and of course the white collar.

'Mr McCann, I presume,' he said, not waiting for a reply nor taking up Martin's offer of a handshake or inviting him inside the front door. 'This must be Charlie.'

When Martin nodded, Bro James put his hand on Charlie's shoulder, turned and said to Martin, 'We'll take care of him from here, Mr McCann.'

Martin's awkward attempt at putting a five pound note into Charlie's top pocket was firmly pushed aside.

'He won't need that here, Mr McCann.'

Bro James, still with his hand on Charlie's shoulder, guided him indoors and firmly closed the door behind him, leaving a disappointed Martin with little choice but to rejoin Digger in the car.

Charlie heard the sound of Digger's car driving off and he cried. Bro James didn't seem to notice as he rang a bell and was immediately joined by a younger brother.

'This is our new recruit Charlie,' he announced. 'Charlie won't give us any trouble, will you?' he stated before walking away.

After such a clinical introduction, followed by his meeting the other twenty-eight first year boys as they were shown to their communal dormitory, Charlie didn't sleep on his first night in Chapel Hill. Every sound, every smell of the country wafting through the dormitory window reminded him of home and he'd have given anything to hear his mother and father talking in the next room, a sound he loved as a child and one he knew he wouldn't hear again for a long time.

As he looked around at the cloistered high ceilings, the shiny floors, and took in the distinct smell of floor polish, it all seemed so unfamiliar and alien, and made him wish like he had never wished before to be back home, a theme that would become familiar throughout his adult life.

But fatigue must have eventually kicked in near morning, for when he was awoken really early by an unmistakeable wake-up bell, the first time he had ever heard such a harsh sound in his young life, he immediately felt overwhelmed with a chronic sense of homesickness. As a child, he had never wanted to stay away overnight anywhere.

But there was no option for Charlie but to remain there, so week followed week, and month followed month and after the initial severe homesickness, Charlie eventually settled at Chapel Hill House. Some brothers were kind, some not so, some were funny, some were not, some patient, some not.

And there was the occasional sarcastic one, who, when handing Charlie back his corrected homework, would simply remark, 'Pity, you could have been good,' or 'There's always India,' a reference to that particular religious order's spreading the faith to the poorer regions of certain countries, where brawn was welcomed when brains were scarce.

Parcels from home were permitted at Halloween. On such occasions, his dear Aunt Maureen, who never did anything by halves, was never found wanting, sending at least four parcels and getting Charlie into all sorts of trouble.

And there was a Visitation Day in the week before Christmas, which always ended up being a bitter-sweet experience for everyone. The glorious anticipation and the joy of his parents' arrival was always more than ably matched by separation anxiety as their time to leave inevitably approached, followed by the dreadful feeling of emptiness when they'd gone.

On the first such visit, with of course the ever-faithful Digger as driver, there was disappointment for Charlie as his father had decided there was too much going on at the farm and entrusted the visit to Maggie, something Charlie wished had been the case on his arrival, but not today. Today he was disappointed, even though it meant he got much more time with his mother.

True to his word to Martin, Digger had got to have his own say, giving Bro James something to think about when he spoke about his nephew.

'Begor, Brother, this is a fine place you have here. I have a nephew at home who could badly do with coming to a place like this.'

Bro James' enquiry regarding the boy's education was firmly met with Digger's delight in explaining that the boy hadn't needed any schooling at all since the arrival of the television in their house.

'There's no knowing all he's learned, Brother, from watching it from when it comes on in the morning to the national anthem being played. I'm very surprised to see there's not even one here!'

Bro James' look of sheer disdain summed up the vast ocean between the two men, bringing a broad smile in a place where smiles were scarce to Charlie's face.

While all the time, Maggie was doing what all good mothers do, fussing over him, asking if he was ok and if he wanted anything, and if he wanted to change his mind, today was the best of all days. By the time they'd get home, it would be too late for Martin to do anything about it. But of course Charlie told her he was fine and would be staying.

Inside he would have given his right arm to come home with them, but he knew that would herald difficulty for his mother at home. And Charlie wouldn't ever do that.

But, as a lover of books and reading, Charlie was aware that he was receiving a good education and had free access to a top class library and other educational supports. He got on well with most of the Brothers, especially Bro Damien, who, realising that Charlie had a keen musical ear, personally trained him before entrusting the baton of the in-house church organ into his young hands whenever he was away.

Charlie had not been trusted like this previously and blossomed in the role. All was well, till he heard a beautiful hymn on his own little radio – another present from Aunt Maureen which he was surprisingly allowed to keep – "Abide with Me". He listened for the same programme on the following week and, sure enough, by the time he'd heard it a few times, he was happy that he had the melody correct both in his head and on his keyboard.

As luck would have it, Bro Damien was going to be away on the following Sunday, and Charlie would get his chance to play the hymn during communion in front of a bigger than usual audience, as there was a religious conference in Chapel Hill on that weekend.

But he hadn't gotten far into it when he saw Bro James walking, but trying to run, towards him, red-faced and waving his hands furiously.

'Stop!' he shouted in a strangled whisper. To a frightened Charlie his voice sounded like a jumbo jet taking off, and he quickly if embarrassedly obeyed.

At the end of Mass, he was told in no uncertain terms that "Abide with Me" had been written by a Scottish man who was an arch enemy of Catholicism, and therefore this hymn was most unsuitable for playing in a Catholic Church.

'I didn't know,' he said apologetically.

'Why didn't you ask?' Bro James shouted at him.

A bit like his farming and hurling brief stints, Charlie felt he could do little right.

48

But, unlike those times, he didn't give up playing the church organ. Charlie had toughened up somewhat.

And on his most recent trip back home, he sensed that his father seemed proud that he had a son "in religious life". For, after Charlie's fourth year in Chapel Hill, he had undertaken temporary vows, was given a black suit and was assigned the religious name of Bro Gerard.

…a young man's awakening…

Charlie's religious and educational progression within the hallowed grounds of Chapel Hill continued undisturbed for another two years. But it was about to be severely challenged. Now aged eighteen and in his Leaving Cert year, Bro Gerard had only imagined the kind of things his peers in the outside world might know about, like girls, relationships or intimacy, even if his mandatory weekly confession was recently taken up with sharing such imaginings.

He had little idea that a decision taken by Bro Damien regarding the upcoming Christmas Concert would provide yet another challenge to his innocent state of mind.

It would be a joint effort between Chapel Hill and the local St Gabriel's Convent, to which all participants' parents would be invited,

Those taking part from both houses would be mostly religious, but, where necessary in the interest of good casting, there would be some lay pupils involved. He announced that he and Sister Teresa would jointly direct the show and Bro Gerard was put forward for an audition by Bro Damien due to his musical ear.

He was initially mortified at his audition to find out there could be girls taking part as well, especially girls not necessarily following the religious path. He tried to share such worries with Bro Damien, but was gently told it was something he'd have to get used to. Privately, he wondered why he would have to get used to this, seeing as how he had already taken a temporary vow of chastity. But the good Brother was not for turning. In fairness, Charlie thought, he was the only member of the order to really see him, hear him, know him and encourage him. So he agreed to give it a try.

Also chosen for a part by Sister Teresa from the paired convent school was a pretty, spirited local girl of seventeen, Marianne McAndrew, who for reasons not quite clear to herself had become fascinated by the young Brothers in the town, young men who had vowed to dedicate their lives to God, just as she had thought about when she was younger.

Over the years, she would occasionally have seen these young Brothers out walking in groups, always in the company of an older religious person, where it was obvious that interaction with the secular community was not encouraged.

Perhaps due to the grief support she had received around the tragic death of her father, she had grown up to be a well-rounded beautiful young girl with a warm smile, a big heart and an educated mind. She liked reading and hearing about people who thought and acted differently than the average and wondered if that might be the reason she liked these young Brothers' minds so much.

She was creative, fun-loving, loved singing and had a bit of a wild streak in her. So, when fate decreed that she would be singing as part of a duet, she thought it sounded like fun.

What if one of these young Brothers were taking part, or better still would be the other half of the duet? It was a long shot, but Sister Teresa had often assured her students that miracles can and do happen.

That thought was nice and seemed even more destined when it was revealed the song for the duet would be "We Dreamed our Dreams", a soulful ballad recently composed by a family friend of Sister Teresa, whose father had written the theme song for the film *The Quiet Man*.

So her disappointment was palpable when a local young man by the name of Neville St John, whom she knew and whom she didn't particularly like, was chosen for the part. A boy who, as her late father might have said, was a bit too fond of himself. But she would still make the most of the occasion.

Incredibly, in the final week of rehearsals, Sister Teresa approached her to say that Mr St John, who was in First Year at college, was struggling to find the time for rehearsals, and would be replaced by someone from within the monastery who had been given the music score for the duet song and was practicing.

Possibility became probability as she prayed in gratitude like she had never prayed before. So, when the change was announced and the replacement was introduced, there stood Bro Gerard, eighteen, tall, fair, blue eyes, extremely shy and a good singer, dressed in black with a white collar. She caught sight of Sister Teresa at the back of the hall and was sure she saw the good nun wink.

And so began what was, for her, the most important connection she had ever made in her short life since her father had passed away. She looked forward to rehearsals like never before. She absolutely loved the duet they were singing, a love song that sadly turned out to be strangely prophetic. *We dreamed our dreams, as we kissed in the summer gladness, but soon I'd cry, it would be goodbye, and you'd be gone. Like the swallows, you'd be gone.*

She had gently but shamelessly encouraged the young Brother to go for a brief walk after rehearsals each night, and when it appeared this was not being noticed, their walks had increased in length, time and meaning.

Whatever problems he had assumed he would encounter when close to a young woman didn't happen with Marianne. Standing close to her during the duet rehearsals gave him not the feared feeling of awkwardness, but a different sensation entirely, one which went a long way to make up for the update from Bro Damien that his mother had written to him in gratitude, but sadly stating they wouldn't be able to attend the concert as it was busy calving time.

Marianne had supported him around that, and of course, being the mischievous lass she now was, she hadn't spared the poor guy during their walks, bombarding him with questions.

Why had he chosen this way of life? Did he not like girls? Did he really think he would be happy for the rest of his life like this?'

She noticed how he reacted to her question about not liking girls, and she liked the reaction. But, of course, she couldn't leave it at that.

So, each night after rehearsal, ignoring the strict condition imposed on Bro Gerard of returning immediately to the monastery after each rehearsal, she encouraged him to walk with her for a while, firstly just around the corner, before extending the walk to the shop at the other side of town which opened late.

They talked, mostly her, about everything. She told him about her father, and he found himself blessed to have had the childhood he had compared to hers. She thought that his childhood sounded idyllic, and Charlie thought there was merit in that analysis. At the end of each such conversation, he always found it hard to pull himself away, such was his joy in her company. There she would buy him a choc ice and noticed how much he would relish such a simple pleasure as they sat by the local river and listened to its uniquely poetical sound.

Then, on one such night's walk, he'd been telling her about his beloved Aunt Maureen, when she leaned over and kissed him on the cheek. His initial innocent blush turned to beetroot red as the strong lights of a car lit them both up in a manner much stronger than their duet spotlight in the concert. It was Bro James.

'Get in!' was all Charlie heard as he quickly abandoned Marianne on the bench.

He was marched quickly and silently to his dormitory. Despite the fear, he still allowed himself to enjoy the memory of that kiss as he fell asleep. The following morning, he was awoken early and summoned to Bro James' office.

'Brother, I could not believe what I witnessed with my own eyes last night. This is possibly the most serious breach of discipline from any novice I have ever witnessed in my time here, and I have given a lot of thought and prayer in trying to come to a decision regarding a suitable response. You have allowed yourself to be caught up in a serious occasion of sin, showing scant regard for your vow of chastity – a clear case for expulsion. However, due to an intercession on your behalf from Bro Damien, you will not be expelled on this occasion.'

Bro James allowed a pause for effect before continuing.

'But it has been decided that the nature of your misdemeanour was such that, in the interest of fairness, a response is demanded, and it is this. You will not be allowed to take any further part in the Christmas Concert rehearsals or in the concert itself. I recommended to Sister Teresa that a similar punishment would be appropriate for Miss McAndrew, but as that young lady has not signed up to any vows, it was your place to remind her that you had. So she has been allowed to continue in the concert.

'I have written a letter to your parents, asking them to collect you the day after tomorrow. You will be going home for a few days to reflect on your actions, which spares them the hardship of getting here for Christmas week, but we expect you back here after Christmas. You are strictly forbidden to ever see or have any contact with Miss McAndrew again. Any further attempts by you to do so will be met with expulsion from our order. Is this understood?'

No words would come to Charlie.

'I asked if that's understood.'

'Yes, Brother,' came in a low voice, slowly and reluctantly.

'Good. We can therefore consider the matter closed for now. You may go.'

...that's what happens when two worlds collide...

As Charlie made his unexpected pre-Christmas trip home in Digger's car, he felt caught somewhere between the joy of going home and the shame of why. He was not to know that things had equally taken a turn back home, until Digger explained the reason why he had been asked to do this particular mission.

'Martin and Maggie are on a mission of their own this morning,' he said, which made Charlie feel somewhat better.

Digger wouldn't elaborate other than to say his parents were expecting an important visitor and that Charlie would find out all when they got home, but right at this minute, Digger's stomach was in bigger need for food than Charlie's curiosity about what was happening at home. And there was no better place to get the best of grub, as Digger called it, than at the cattle mart in Kilkenny where Digger could also find out the current price for weanling calves.

When they eventually got home, his father and mother were still waiting for their visitor. Martin was sitting at the window, the one Charlie had looked out while waiting to be brought to Chapel Hill for the first time, his fingers tapping on the kitchen table in time to an aimless tune he was humming. Charlie had good reason to be familiar with that particular coping skill of his father's, for it often heralded trouble.

Maggie hugged her son and thanked Digger who, reading the situation, said he had to keep going as he had jobs to do. Martin immediately offered Charlie to help Digger, which Charlie suspected was to keep him from witnessing the expected visitor. Be that as it may, Charlie was happy to assure Digger he would be along as soon as he had changed his clothes. When Martin went outside to talk to Digger, Maggie proceeded to fill Charlie in about his estranged Uncle Jack who had recently been diagnosed with a serious illness and wanted to return home for Christmas and make peace with his brother.

While Charlie was putting on working clothes, Maggie smilingly told him she had his favourite currant cake baked for his homecoming.

Digger drove off and Martin came back to his window seat and his humming. Charlie set out to do what he had been told, but once out of sight, he suddenly decided that he would like to know about this mysterious uncle. So he did an out-of-sight U-turn.

He was just in time to hear his father say to his mother, 'You seem awful anxious for that fellow to arrive.'

'He's your brother and I think it's right that he should come to his childhood home, if that's what he wants to do.'

'You don't know the story.' Martin sounded so angry, enough to put fear into Charlie.

But his mother's voice remained calm.

'I don't care about the story. That was then, now is now. Let him come home. But I suppose what I think or say doesn't much matter here.'

'You always had your say here.'

'Oh sure, like I had my say about what we'd have for dinner, what colour the kitchen should be painted or what Mass we'd go to, but when it came to important things within this house, I never had any say.'

'What do you mean?'

Maggie's voice now broke.

'I'll never forget the way I felt, the day Charlie left here. He looked out the back window of Digger's car as ye pulled out of the yard. He was crying. Every fibre in my being wanted to drag him out of that car and wrap my arms around him. He was only thirteen, Martin. Thirteen, for God's sake! It tore the heart out of me!'

Listening, Charlie had to stifle tears at this point.

Martin was quiet for a second, then said, 'Why didn't you say something?'

'For the same reason I never say anything. You decide everything, Martin. Just because young Charlie was impressed by a Brother who came to his school the week before he finished primary school, you immediately made plans with the school principal. And before I could say Chapel Hill, it was all arranged. You never talked to me about it. You never talk to me about anything!'

At this point, Charlie decided he was hearing perhaps too much, so he decided to go help Digger after all. But just then, a fancy-looking Volkswagen car pulled into the yard and his curiosity was aroused once more, so he told himself another few minutes wouldn't do Digger any harm. He wanted at least to catch a look at his apparently famous Uncle Jack in this fabulous car.

He spied his mother brushing the flour from her pinafore with the back of her hand as she went to greet him at the door. So, he thought, this is my Uncle Jack, who looks to be a completely different kind of man than any I have met so far, and he liked what he saw. Jack was tall with an air of artistic flair, well-dressed but pale. He wore navy slacks, a blue shirt with a cravat and a tweed sports jacket.

'Jack, I presume?' Maggie held out her hand.

'Jack it is, I believe you're Maggie. It's nice to meet you, Maggie.'

'It's nice to meet you, Jack. I like the car.'

'It's a hired car, Maggie.'

'Be that as it may, it's as welcome as you are.'

All this politeness didn't seem to go down too well with Martin.

'It's time enough you're meeting her, and if I had my say or my way, you would never have met her. Will you look at the get-up of this fella, not to mention that car. This is a small village cottage, one you deserted, not some fancy hotel!'

'Martin, take it easy,' Maggie pleaded.

'So, you're taking his side already. By Jesus it didn't take him long to win you over.'

'No one's won over and there are no sides any more. The British are gone, Martin. Your father and uncle are gone. Let them rest in peace.'

His father's voice became raised. 'You weren't there. You know nothing of what 'twas like in our house when this traitor joined the British Army. My uncle, God rest him, said at the time that he wished the Brits had shot him, that he would have died a hero. Instead he lived in shame all his life, never once going outside the door till the day he died. My father maybe less so, but he had reared the pair of us well with the few bob he had scraped together working with another British bastard! But he said all of that was nothing compared to how he felt when this, the only one of us with a brain, stabbed him in the back.'

Charlie's jaw dropped.

'Martin's right,' Jack said to Maggie. 'He tells the story accurately, just as it was.'

Martin was unimpressed.

'You needn't think you'll soft-soap me or Maggie with your British charm.'

'If you don't mind, I'll speak for myself,' Maggie replied. 'Jack, you're very welcome in this house.'

'If that's how you want it, you can have him!'

Martin stormed away from the house in the direction away from Charlie. Charlie, thanking his lucky stars, decided he maybe had heard enough, so he high-tailed it to Digger's house before his father might decide to do the same ahead of him.

And thankfully, as in most things in life, Martin had showed his softer side on the following day and Jack was allowed to spend Christmas Day at the family home. The healing had begun, primarily for Jack but perhaps for all. Charlie was allowed to spend time with Jack as they shared their respective stories, which fascinated both parties equally.

So, when it came to Charlie's return to Chapel Hill, Uncle Jack decided to save Digger and Martin a trip and announced that he would like to do the chauffeuring. Martin wasn't sure, but eventually the busyness on the farm in that week sealed the deal, which pleased Charlie no end.

And so they arrived at Chapel Hill on a frosty Dec 27th, 1970 in Jack's hired Volkswagen, where they were initially greeted warmly by one of the younger Brothers, who said he would look after Charlie. But Jack requested a meeting with Bro James and insisted that Charlie would remain for the conversation. Bro James was not impressed with the fact he had no notice of what he called an irregularity, and like Martin before him, Jack was not invited indoors.

'Good morning, Brother,' Jack said, 'I am proud to be this young man's uncle.'

To which Bro James replied, 'This is not a drop-in centre.'

If Jack was thrown by this coldness, it didn't show.

'Yes, Brother, I know that, but what I have to say is important.'

'If it's that important, why didn't his parents speak to me themselves?'

'They're busy people, Brother, trying to eke out a living from a small parcel of land-commission land and a handful of cows, so they've delegated this particular task to me.'

Bro James immediately protested at the boy's presence, stating that it would be much more appropriate for the two adults to have the conversation alone.

The mutual disregard between the two men was immediately obvious as Jack continued.

'I feel it important that Charlie be present.'

Bro James's protracted silence was taken as a go-ahead by Jack.

'The McCann family feel it's important to let you know how deeply unhappy we are about a few recent decisions you've made about the lad and thought a conversation might be beneficial.'

'Beneficial to whom?' was the reply.

'Hopefully all parties might, shall we say, be more enlightened.'

Bro James raised his voice. 'I'm a very busy man.'

With a wide sweep of his hand, Jack took in the entire monastery building.

'I can imagine. Keeping young boys in their place must be heavy work.'

The haughty approach of Bro James was unyielding.

'I sincerely hope you don't think that I'm going to discuss monastic disciplinary policy with you.'

'See, that's where we are different, Brother. You want to talk about monastic disciplinary policy, while I want to talk about a young boy's wellbeing.'

Bro James raised his tone another notch. 'Let me assure you, Mr McCann, I have no intention of discussing any individual case with you.'

'Oh, I think you will, Brother. See, you are not dealing here with one of your typical Irish parents, who innocently give you unquestioned power of attorney over their young sons' lives and formation.'

Bro James seemed temporarily stopped in his tracks.

'Strong with the weak, Brother, and weak with the strong, eh?' was Jack's response to the silence, as he continued. 'Good, now in your own time, you might try and explain to me how you justified denying this young boy his first and possibly his last opportunity to be on stage as part of what would have been a magical moment.'

'Because he has already had his magical moment, conducting an improper relationship with a young girl from this town.'

'Surely there's little point in expecting a young boy to take a vow of chastity unless he has some idea what it is that he's actually giving up. That's all the poor boy was doing, a little bit of harmless research, so to speak.'

Bro James puffed up his chest.

'I will not be preached to in my own monastery by a man I don't know and who has not had the decency to seek a proper appointment to see me.'

Jack had travelled too far for too long to be browbeaten by a man of the cloth, but decided once more to appeal to Bro James's better nature.

'I implore you, Brother, give young Charlie a second chance.'

Bro James's temperature was visibly rising now.

'Firstly, Bro Gerard has already been replaced in the concert programme, so it's too late. Secondly he is no longer "young Charlie" as you refer to him. He is now Bro Gerard, a religious brother with a temporary sworn vow of chastity.'

Jack remained unruffled. 'Surely the word temporary means "trial"?'

'It means a probationary period,' an angry Bro James replied. 'One which he has already clearly failed. It was an instant expulsion matter, so you should be pleased at my sense of fairness and leniency in reflecting on this matter for a further week and allowing Bro Gerard to do the same.'

Bro James's continuing patronising and defensive attitude in this matter now sadly steered Jack off-script.

'Fair and fear can never go in the same sentence, Brother. Just tell me this. Do you honestly think it's right to lock a thirteen-year-old child in here, so that he'll never know the world in which he lives, until he is trapped into taking vows of poverty, chastity and obedience? And what will he want them for? By the time you're finished with the poor chap, he's never going to own anything, he'll be terrified of anything to do with a woman, and even more petrified of disobeying an authoritarian tyrant like you!'

Bro James silently turned and retreated indoors, bringing a frightened Charlie with him.

But Jack had to have the last word.

'Go on, Brother, hide away behind your cold stone walls, but mark my word, the days of your stone walls are numbered.'

While Jack was rolling this one last throw of the dice, Charlie was already planning his own last throw of his own dice. Having been greatly encouraged by all that Uncle Jack had to say to Bro James, he felt it right that he should write to Marianne, explaining his absence from the concert rehearsals and the concert itself.

Marianne's address was easy to find due to her aunt Julie's shop being well known and his knowing that her mother worked there. So, on the following day, he did write to her, shared his feelings with her and hoped she would meet him one more time at a named destination so that he could explain everything properly to her. He had a card of stamps hidden in his locker, a present from Aunt Maureen, and felt good as he popped the letter into the post box outside the monastery.

Sadly, it was Maria, Marianne's mother, who picked up the letter while the young lady was on an errand, and having decided it was her duty to check letters to her daughter, she opened it. After a brief glance, it didn't take her long to take it straight to Bro James. Charlie was immediately removed from his peers to be alone in the meditation wing of the monastery and while Bro James awaited the arrival of the new Provincial General to formally decide what was to become of the young Bro Gerard, Martin and Maggie awaited the final verdict.

It didn't take long.

In the midst of a few late Christmas cards, the postman handed Maggie one letter that didn't seem like a card. Maggie instantly recognised the monastery envelope and called in Martin before nervously opening it, fearing the worst.

Dec 30th, 1970

Dear Mr. & Mrs. McCann,

It is with deep regret that I inform you of Charlie's expulsion from our Order and Chapel Hill House.

His expulsion is due to his continued defiance of our Rules, and in particular his improper relationship with a local girl, which culminated in him sending a wholly inappropriate letter to her last week, without our knowledge or approval.

I will personally bring Charlie home next Monday morning, Jan 4th. Please expect us about 8am. He will be dressed in secular clothes, his parting present from the Order.

God Bless
Brother James O'Connell

So, Charlie was taken away from Chapel Hill House for the last time in the black early morning darkness that only a dreary January can bring, just a little over a week after Uncle Jack's visit to the monastery. Bro James had chosen to chauffeur the black Ford Anglia himself, which worried Charlie as he was silently invited to sit in the rear. And in a case of reverse irony, he was as heartbroken now as he had been coming here six years previously.

He had often longed to come home permanently, but not under these circumstances. And he definitely no longer felt he belonged in his own village, that's if he ever did. Even more worrying was his thought that perhaps, apart from his mother, the same could be said for his home. Added to that was the suffocating feeling that he was unlikely to ever see Marianne McAndrew again, seeing as how she had chosen not to meet him as he had asked in his letter.

But he equally knew he could not afford the luxury of feeling sorry for himself. He needed to focus, to be prepared for the inevitable upset and shame that would greet him on his arrival home, and there's nothing that helps focus the mind more than fear, fear that was growing within him with each passing mile.

In this new world of fading hope, Charlie had two hopes left within him, that his uncle Jack would still be at home and that Bro James wouldn't come into the house. Almost as if reading his mind, Bro James unceremoniously dashed the second of those hopes when he announced that he would be briefly coming in to speak to his parents, despite Charlie saying he would be fine just being dropped off at the cross near his home.

When the torturously silent journey eventually ended, they were met at the door by Maggie, who warmly hugged Charlie. Inside, sitting as usual at the rear window, was

64

Martin who stood when they came into the kitchen, and pointed to a seat for Bro James, who declined. The seeming absence of Jack was Charlie's first hope dashed.

'We meet again, Brother, but I wish the circumstances were different,' Martin said.

'We all wish they were different, Mr McCann.'

Maggie wasn't quite so accommodating. 'So, what did Charlie do that was so terrible that he had to be taken away from what was his home for the past six years like a thief in the night?'

The reply was clinical and cold. 'It's our policy.'

Maggie wasn't done. 'I think it's a sad policy that demands that a young boy be sent home in the middle of his Leaving Cert year.'

'We did of course consider this.'

'But obviously not enough,' Maggie replied.

With that, Bro James took a letter from his inside pocket.

'Perhaps this will explain our actions better than any words of mine.'

As he began to take the letter from its envelope, shivers of fear overcame Charlie as he recognised his letter to Marianne, so much so that he thought of running, but his father's voice stopped him in his tracks.

'Stay where you are.'

Bro James began to read out Charlie's letter.

'Hello to the one bright spark in my otherwise miserable world. Marianne, you have no idea how differently I see the world since I met you at the concert rehearsals. A thousand blessings on Brother Damien for selling the idea of a joint concert to Sister Teresa and another thousand on the good Sister for buying it! I am heartbroken that they won't allow us any further contact. If my memory is correct, the final concert rehearsal is tomorrow night. I will pretend I'm sick and request to remain in my room, sneak out the bedroom window and wait for you at the railway bridge between six o'clock and rehearsal time. If there's any way you can get

out, even for a few minutes, I will be there. They think they have me trapped here, but they won't keep me from seeing the one person who gives meaning to my life. I am so happy I have found you, whatever the price will be.'

Bro James sarcastically concluded his reading of the letter by stating, 'It's signed with two x's, whatever those stand for.'

The long silence, which seemed like an eternity to the exposed Charlie, was broken only by the ticking of the mantlepiece enamel alarm clock, another legacy of Aunt Maureen, till there came the sound of a slow handclap from outside the room, but increasing in volume till Jack entered and the clapping was replaced by an awkward silence.

If Charlie was delighted at his intervention, Martin seemed unsure and Maggie, almost automatically, altered her stance to that of mediator.

Jack addressed Bro James in a steely tone. 'We meet again, Brother.'

Bro James didn't answer. But Jack had something to say whether the good Brother wanted to hear it or not

'Well done, Brother,' Jack began, 'on tearing this young man's world to shreds, desecrating his heartfelt beautifully-crafted love letter to the lucky young lady involved.' He winked at Charlie in a quietly affirmative way. 'And in case you were wondering, Brother, the applause was for Charlie's courage and writing skills. I'm sure you thought it was for you, for it must give you a great feeling of power, watching a young boy's private thoughts, hopes and dreams being ripped asunder, here in the one place where he was entitled to feel safe, in his own home. Seemingly, your endless quest for power is never satisfied. Not happy with dragging the poor chap home in the middle of the night, you felt the need to totally humiliate him.'

If Bro James was disturbed by this, he didn't show it.

'Even though he can no longer be part of our order, I felt I owed it to him to teach him one final harsh lesson, that all actions have consequences. I'm sure Mr McCann' – he nodded towards Martin – 'will agree with me on this matter, and I sincerely hope this lesson will stand him in good stead wherever he goes in life.'

Martin continued to remain silent, but Jack had at this point little interest in silence.

'There's a fine line between teaching a boy a lesson and breaking him. You may just have destroyed that young man's whole life with that demolition job.'

Bro James' face began to turn an unholy tone of red, which matched his voice.

'You came back here to gain favour with your sister-in-law and your nephew, and I must admit it seems like you have done a good job. I'm sure, in their immature eyes, you look like some kind of folk hero. You see, men like you are all too plentiful in this fast becoming Godforsaken secular world, where the only God is prestige and short-term connections are based on charismatic charm, where honesty is a disposable quality, where there's more to be gained from the wickedness of the lie. Your brother strikes me as a man of good sense, a man who will see you for who and what you are. I'm sure he already feels quite inadequate because of your presence here.'

Jack went quiet for a time, but not for long.

'You couldn't be further from the truth, Brother. Martin is ten times the man I am or ever could be. He knows that. Young Charlie knows it. Maggie knows it, and as sure as hell, I know it. The only advantage I may have over him in this present situation is that I have managed, rightly or wrongly, to live outside this sterile controlling culture for a great number of years, and as a result, I have a mind of my own.'

Bro James at this point threw his eyes to heaven.

'Congratulations! I hope it serves young Charlie well.'

'It can hardly serve him any worse than the mind which has landed this boy home on his hard-working parents barely a week after Christmas, with his education unfinished. Where in God's name are they going to find a school for him now at this time of the year?'

The silence that followed only inspired Jack.

'You talk about the wickedness of the secular world. Well, let me tell you, Brother, you should be far more concerned about the wickedness such as this that's deeply imbedded in your monastery and others like it, and that is the wickedness of silence, where control is the key, fear is the master, and all natural curiosity and desires are suffocated in guilt.'

Maggie interjected as mediator.

'Jack, leave it.'

'Very wise, Mrs McCann,' Bro James said. 'I'm surprised that neither you nor your husband have intervened sooner in what's been an outrageous attack on me and my order within your home.'

Charlie could feel the fear rising within him as his father slowly stood to his feet, looked at him for what seemed like forever, then switched his gaze to Bro James.

'To tell you the truth, Brother, I'm a bit surprised myself. But as I listened to all that was being said this morning, maybe my eyes have been opened. I'm a simple hard-working man and I haven't it all figured out in my head yet. But one thing I'm agreeing with you on is the fact that I did allow what you call an irreverent attack to be made in this house.'

'I accept your apology, Mr McCann.'

But Martin hadn't finished.

'Bro James, this irreverent attack was made by *you*. Jack is right, you had no right to read the boy's private letter here in front of us to justify what you refer to as your policy. You had no right to decide for me as to how I should think about or how I would handle my brother. I'll not deny he has changed a few things around here, the way people see

68

things. I'm a slow man to accept change, but I think I could get to like one or two of these changes.

'We mightn't have your power, Brother, but we have something which you will never have. We have family. Jack is part of that family and will remain so whether he decides to stay or returns to his home in England, as is Charlie. I should have listened to Maggie and trusted my instincts on the evening I left him with you six years ago and I can see that now.'

Coming to Charlie and putting his hand on his shoulder, Martin continued.

'I'm sorry, Charlie, I didn't act then, but I am now.' He turned his focus again on Bro James. 'Brother, you have your morning's work done. You have rid your order of another troublesome young boy, so go back to Chapel Hill and we'll look after young Charlie from here.'

Maggie immediately went to Martin and Charlie's side in a display of family unity, leaving a clearly shocked Bro James with no more to do than look at each of them in turn, as he moved towards the door.

'I bid you all farewell,' was his final word, but not Maggie's.

'Would you mind leaving the letter, Brother. After all, it is Charlie's private property.'

As the shocked man of the cloth reluctantly handed the letter to Charlie, it seemed right that the final words of a meeting that had turned from disaster to triumph for Charlie should come from the young man himself.

'Told you that you should have let me off at the cross.'

…conversations on a homecoming…

Despite that beautiful moment of family unity, acceptance and redemption, young Charlie found post monastery life strange, as he tried to re-adjust to the outside world. His home was still home, but his young heart was aching for the person he had to leave behind. But at least now he understood why she hadn't shown at the railway bridge on that evening. Did Marianne even know now about his letter to her? Would she ever?

Getting into a Leaving Cert class in January was not easy, so the nearest secondary school to his home was quickly chosen for convenience, wherein two of his best subjects were not being taught. His Leaving Cert results the following August reflected this, when he got honours in just two subjects: Irish and Latin, which sadly were insufficient to gain him a university scholarship. So another dream, college education, died, and he was gently reminded by Martin of the necessity to find a job.

Then a break. A vacancy had arisen in the expanding store department in the local creamery, of which Charlie's father was a committee member. When the creamery manager, Mr Larry Broderick, met Charlie on the street accidentally and asked if he'd be interested, Charlie gladly showed huge interest. But, being true to his authentic self, Martin thought it would be better if the job was properly advertised, interviews held, and the best person chosen for the job. Happily, Charlie was that person, meaning Martin maintained his integrity and Maggie got a few extra pounds from Charlie's wages each week, so everything was better for everyone.

Better still, Mr Broderick seemed to recognise something in Charlie and encouraged it, especially Charlie's love of reading and writing. Over a period of time, he shared with Charlie his own humble beginnings, helping on a delivery truck for his own local creamery when he was Charlie's age, graduating in time to being the lorry driver, proudly adding that this was in the days before power-steering. He had signed up for evening college classes, liked and pursued college education, achieved a degree in agriculture, and here he was.

Around that time the same Mr Broderick was also spearheading an effort to secure an outreach Diploma in Social Studies programme for the village. This would be delivered by University College Cork, part-time over two years, in evening classes at one of the local schools. The quest was a success and a willing Charlie, delighted that he would get to college after all, even if it was a slightly different route, signed up. The creamery paid for his course, the money to be taken back, over the two years, from his wages.

And Larry, which by now he had asked Charlie to call him, kept a few greyhounds, one of which was showing promise and could do with an evening dog-walker, for which of course Charlie would be paid. His life suddenly seemed to take on meaning again.

Bro James however had been right about one thing. Uncle Jack did get itchy feet a month after Charlie's homecoming and returned to his home in England, which was quickly and cruelly followed by his Aunt Maureen's sudden departure from this life due to chronic heart failure.

He'd been at evening class the night Maureen passed and had arrived home on his bicycle, the light of which was yet another present from the same Aunt Maureen, shortly after ten o'clock to find a large crowd of neighbours outside of his parents' home on a fine April night. As he tried to figure out what was happening, he noticed that as he cycled closer towards the neighbours, they parted silently like the Red Sea before him, leading him to know something serious had occurred.

Then his mother, with tears in her eyes, came towards him, and Charlie would never forget the power of the five simple words she used to convey the bad news.

'The fun is over, Charlie.'

Charlie instantly knew what was behind that simple line, words of brevity and beauty and a shining example of the old maxim that sometimes less is more. For there had always been fun whenever Maureen was around.

On the next day, when the parish priest asked Maggie if she had any special wish regarding the funeral mass of her sister, she remembered something she'd heard Maureen saying to a priest in the hospital who had asked her the same question before saying Mass. 'In the name of God, Father, don't keep us all day.' And all that knew her, including the priest, knew that she would have enjoyed that, and to his credit the priest who knew Maureen took no offence.

But life carried on, as did his job and studies, and a few years later, he graduated with flying colours. The highlight of his post-monastery life was undoubtedly the graduation ceremony in Cork University, even if the dark grey buildings reminded him somewhat of Chapel Hill.

Charlie's social life was slow to develop, perhaps as a legacy of his monastery days. At some point he ventured to a few of the local pubs with Marty, and to one or two dances, but the bright lights and loud music were not his scene, and before he knew it, Charlie was twenty-two and socially adrift.

…it will happen when you least expect it…

He didn't like late night loudness or brightness and had decided that a particular dance (Joe Dolan) would be his last for a while. That was the night when he noticed Vera who, like him, seemed a little ill at ease and didn't seem to be asked to dance too often. He continued to observe her and liked how she was not trying to draw attention to herself. She struck him as being naturally pretty looking, with little make-up and what seemed like clips in her long straight brown hair, the kind of look that appealed to him. Not being any kind of expert in this area, he deemed her to be the same age as himself. After spending so many years in a monastery, the "quiet girl" image seemed to fit.

He asked her to dance and was almost shocked when she agreed. He observed that she seemed to be the perfect height for him as they exchanged the usual "do you come here often" conversation. And, as was customary at the time, if you liked the girl, you asked for a second dance, especially when it was a "slow dance", which it was and he did. She again nodded, which was another first for Charlie. And so the courtship with Vera began and began well. She seemed more contemplative than other girls her age, which suited him. This, he discovered, might be at least partly due to her beloved father's passing only eight months previously. By now Marty had his own car and was happy to loan it to Charlie, so long as he brought it back full of petrol. Vera preferred weekend trips over public houses, which again suited Charlie.

If Vera was quiet, her extended family were very outgoing, welcoming and entertaining, and quickly he became part of that family. When Vera and he announced their engagement a year later, no one was too surprised. And no one had any doubts about the great couple they would make.

But at their engagement party, he himself realised that he was beginning to entertain doubts, as much about his own sense of readiness for a lifetime commitment more than anything in particular about Vera. Such thoughts continued to trouble him, but not trusting his judgement of matters of this kind, Charlie went along with the tide of social pressure and before he knew it, the wedding was being planned for the following July. Month speedily followed month and all too soon it was June, and Charlie recognised a growing sense of panic that could no longer be ignored.

Then an opportunity presented itself perhaps for him to take charge of the situation. A priest originally from Vera's parish, who had served all his life in an American diocese, had recently retired back home and was acting as an associated pastor to the Parish Priest who had been booked to conduct the marriage ceremony. Surely this man of God with experience of a more secular world would understand and support his view that the right thing might be to call the wedding off, and that this man might also make the awkward task of informing Vera's Parish Priest of this decision somewhat easier.

So he made an appointment to meet the returned padre, an appointment that quickly ended in disappointment. Having listened to Charlie's story, the good padre assured him that he was only suffering from similar cold feet as he himself had experienced a few weeks prior to his own ordination. His own resistance to God's plan back then was as wrong as Charlie's was now. He convinced Charlie that all wedding plans should go ahead.

With that, the meeting was over, and Charlie was alone again, just as he was when Marianne hadn't shown at the bridge, just as he was in Bro James' car on his way home from the monastery, once again surrounded by shame.

Coming from a background of strong religious influences, (*Anyone who sets his hand on the plough and changes his mind is not fit for the kingdom of God*), Charlie decided to follow the pastor's advice, and a few days later, went to his own Parish Priest for his ironically named "freedom to marry" papers. Now there was no turning back and, even if he still had some doubts, he approached the marriage almost martyr-like, for if there was one thing Charlie knew a lot about from his religious studies, it was martyrs.

And so, aged just twenty-four, Charlie was married to Vera, and within the year, Mary Elizabeth was born. And when he first held her, he experienced a feeling like nothing else this world can offer. He had never felt happier in his entire life and could totally see what the associated pastor was talking about in terms of what was meant to be.

… almost persuaded…

Five years had passed since Bro Gerard's disappearance from her life. Marianne McAndrew was by now aged twenty-three and had developed into a beautiful young woman in all respects. She lived with her mother and worked as manager in the town's art, craft and hobby shop, owned by her Aunt Julie, where her mother had previously worked when she was a child.

That young Brother occasionally came into her mind. Such memories were hard to avoid with the towering monastery casting its long shadow everywhere. The memory was especially triggered one day when a poster appeared in a local window about the upcoming regional finals of a popular drama festival being staged, for one night only, in a town hall, fifteen miles from where they lived. She found herself immediately being interested when she noticed that one of the drama groups, from a village she felt certain Charlie had told her he was from, was performing a new one act play written by a Charlie McCann.

She remembered once asking Bro Gerard about his surname, and she was pretty sure that he said McCann, because she remembered them agreeing about the similarity between their respective surnames, but now she was kicking herself that she had never enquired about his former first name.

Neville, her partner, was away on one of his business trips, so she told her story to her aunt, who agreed to drive her there.

'Sure, I love plays anyway, so it doesn't matter to me who wrote it.'

But it did matter to Marianne. It mattered a lot.

Neville, yes, the same Neville St John, her singing duet partner from the Christmas concert rehearsals of 1970, was now sales manager for a local agricultural engineering company and was often away overnight.

So, how did she end up with this guy that she had considered a bit too full of himself? The story is as old as time. He had persistently pursued her, and his persistence paid off.

Initially she had not given Neville half as much attention as he'd been giving her. But, in time, she agreed to go out with him. Her female friends said she'd be mad not to.

'He's good-looking,' they argued. 'He's successful, he's a muscly rugby player, and he's building his own home.'

One night shortly afterwards, when he kissed her in the new house he had brought her to see, she suddenly became excited at the idea of getting away from her mother and living "in sin" in this fine house. And so the deed was done.

What Neville failed to tell her that night, or any other night, was that his mother, who lived next door to the new house, was not easy to be around, someone who wasn't slow to let anyone and everyone who came into her path know what she thought about them. Marianne felt her disapproval the minute they'd finally been introduced, a full year into their relationship.

When Neville said that Marianne worked in an art shop, the look on his mother's face matched the patronising tone in her voice as she repeated in a monotone half-sentence, 'Arti-farty and works in a shop,' leaving Marianne in no doubt as to what she thought of that.

Despite Neville's repeated, 'Ah, don't mind her,' Marianne was uneasy at his mother's disapproval. Remembering what her own mother had endured in the arena of disapproval, she didn't feel it was the correct path for her. But on a night away on the following weekend, when he asked her to move in with him when the house would be finished, she found that her excitement at that prospect seemed to far outweigh any doubts she was having. Once they would be living together, she thought, the mother would hopefully stay out of her life and their lives, and in due course they would get married.

The house was finished six months later, and Marianne moved in with Neville. And it began well enough until it came to buying furniture and fittings for their new home. Unknown to Marianne, Neville's mother was appointed to that particular task, and she came home from work one evening to find that it was practically all in place. Surprising as it was to her, it was no surprise at all to Neville who felt it was such an obvious decision, seeing that his mother had been highly trained as an interior designer in her younger days. For peace sake, Marianne decided to let it go, but she regretted it, as the house never felt like it was her own.

...all life's a stage...

When Mr Broderick started up an amateur drama group in the village, he encouraged Charlie to join their ranks for their first scheduled production of a one-act play called *The Glorious Uncertainties of the Turf*.

Again, it seemed the universe was speaking to both Larry, whose love of greyhounds was legendary, and to Charlie who would be playing the part of a loveable gambler and perpetual loser, whose wife wanted him to give up his gambling ways. Having honestly seen himself as someone who was addicted to possibilities, the part seemed made for him. He knew it would involve late nights and some Sunday rehearsals, which Vera wouldn't be keen on.

And perhaps it's fair to reflect and ask who could blame her? After all, she had a small child to mind all day while Charlie was at work, especially when the play proved popular and was invited to go on a mini-tour to the local village halls. When it all came to its end, Charlie decided, in fairness to all, that he would step away from the stage for now.

But when Mr Broderick's promising greyhound (Log Cabin) began fulfilling that promise and got to the final of one of the major cups in Shelbourne Park, Larry organised a bus to bring all the drama group and their wives to the evening, especially Charlie, who had been very involved in a lot of the walking of Log Cabin, and his wife, but Vera declined the offer.

If Larry was a generous and kind man in general, he wasn't as generous when it came to giving out tips for any race in which any of his dogs were running. He loved everything to do with greyhounds but didn't believe in gambling and didn't think anyone else should either.

'Did you ever see a poor bookie?' was his reflective question, followed by the salutary, 'Anything can happen in a dog race.'

But on that night, when Log Cabin won, there was no more decent man on the way home, and a truly great night for food and beverages was had by all till the wee hours.

So, when Charlie was encouraged to write an original one act play for the group's next production, his ego was stroked again and, once more, he forgot his promise to Vera. His rationale was that things would be better at home this time, for he had written a part in his play, *Chains of Freedom*, especially for Mary Elizabeth who was now aged seven. This would mean that Vera could attend all the rehearsals so this play would be more about family unity than division. By now, they had purchased a small but practical car and Charlie would get a lift to rehearsals, so Vera could come and go as she pleased. But she chose to continue to remain at home to, 'clean the house properly while ye're not in it.'

Apart from that setback, rehearsals for this play were an incredible experience for Charlie. Having Mary Elizabeth with him was great, as was seeing the fruits of his imagination taking shape on the rehearsal stage, and to truly feel and hear from the cast that the play was really good.

The play successfully navigated all the preliminary rounds and, against all odds for a new play, made its way to the regional semi-final and won. There was much praise from the judges for the courage of the group to take on an original play and for the writer's craft. And, when Mary Elizabeth got a very special mention, the same Larry Broderick carried her on his shoulders up the entire hall and onto the stage, which brought tears to Charlie's eyes.

But a brilliant night came to a shuddering halt when they got home and found the house in darkness. As Charlie frantically opened the door to see if Vera was ok, he saw a letter on the table with his name on it. While pretending to

80

open and scan the contents, he quickly reassured Mary Elizabeth that her granny, her mam's mam, had taken ill and that Vera was spending the night with her.

Charlie put on the heat, dished up the fish & chips he had bought on the way home, and reminded Mary Elizabeth that, as tomorrow was Saturday and he wasn't working, she could sleep as long as she liked in the morning. He told her how proud he was of her before she went to her bed, and in no time at all, he could hear that she was sound asleep.

It was then he sat down to read Vera's letter and his heart sank as he read what it said. For someone who had little interest in his writing and resented his whole involvement in the drama group, even with Mary Elizabeth involved, she had for some unexplained reason chosen to read *Chains of Freedom* earlier that day for the first time.

Dealing with the apparent contradiction between winning on stage but losing at home, Charlie's mind was addled and he found it hard to sleep. But he was happy that Mary Elizabeth slept soundly, so much so that she didn't stir till eleven o'clock the following morning. When she eventually emerged from her room still with a sleepy head, she chatted to him as she was eating her breakfast about the excitement of the previous night, highlighting her being carried up through the hall on Mr Broderick's shoulders as something she would never forget. If she was upset about her mother being away, she didn't say.

Going to her mother's was something Vera did frequently, whenever she felt she needed space. Charlie had arranged for their childminder to take care of Mary Elizabeth for a few hours that afternoon as he set sail to Vera's mother's house, to face the music once more.

All the joy he had felt last night, the involvement of their daughter and the pride that came with winning, seemed to be entirely insufficient at best, and irrelevant at worst, in the face of the fear he felt as he approached. He never could deal very well with the tension Vera could create whenever they were having a disagreement.

On reflection, perhaps this was one of the shadow-reasons he had decided to go ahead with the wedding. As he anxiously made his way there, he found himself silently arguing with God, the universe or whatever higher power would listen to his pleas. *Why does it have to be this hard? You and I had a deal, remember? I'd do the right thing and marry Vera, you'd help, and if she was happy, that was all I wanted in return. But you can see for yourself how bloody well that's turned out. Not alone is she's so obviously unhappy, she actually feels her unhappiness lies entirely at my door, which means neither of us are happy, and I'm getting seriously worried about the impact of all of this on our daughter's happiness and wellbeing.*

He approached Vera's mother's front door with anxiety, and it was warranted.

'Is that what you're planning?' was the doorstep greeting as Vera waved a copy of his play in his face.

'You know the way my creative mind works,' he said with little hope.

'I know only too well,' she replied. 'So, who is she? How long? God, I've been so blind, or in denial, fooling myself, hoping I was wrong. But I'm not wrong, Charlie, am I?'

'Actually, Vera, you are wrong,' he said, surprised at his calmness, probably based on a potential loophole in his wife's interpretation of his play.

'Don't lie to me, Charlie. It seems you've spent a long time lying to me.'

'Is that what you thought the play was really about?'

'What else could it be about?' she screamed at him. 'It's set in a flat in London where a married man and his young daughter have come to stay with his new woman. What else did you expect me to believe?'

Charlie remained calm.

'Did you read the play to the end?' he asked.

82

'No. I didn't need to and I certainly didn't want to!'

'That's a pity,' he said.

'Why?'

'Well, if you had read it to the end, you would have seen for yourself that the play ends with it all being a dream, a bad dream that had become a nightmare. When the guy in the play wakes up in his own bed, with his wife alongside him, and their daughter safely in her own room, and he realises that everything at home had remained exactly as it was, he is so relieved and happy that it was just that, a bad dream.'

If he thought that would have rescued the situation, he was mistaken. Vera's facial expression hadn't changed one iota as she listened to Charlie's happy-ever-after narrative.

'Why was he having such dreams in the first place? Answer me that!'

And, as the character Miley in the TV series *Glenroe* once remarked, *There's no answer to that.*

But as he drove home, Charlie's head was not in a great place and his thoughts returned to what had been the motivation behind that play in the first place.

He had also felt pretty sure for some time that Vera possibly suffered some kind of underlying emotional issues and when she had eventually agreed to see the doctor from her own village, there was no doubt from how the doctor greeted Vera that he had known her from before and that they had discussed such issues previously. But again, even with the doctor's recommendation, Vera refused to consider medication.

…when art imitates life…

Marianne McAndrew's live-in experience with her boyfriend turned out to be a million miles from what she had envisaged. Neville seemed to spend most of his free time either down at the local rugby club or with his mother. The occasional mention of marriage and family was met with a shrug of the shoulders or a change of conversation.

And so the template for their living together had been laid down and Marianne wondered why she had given up her youth, her beauty and all she had to offer to this unappreciative man, who treated her like a trophy girlfriend, very happy to have her on his arm at business and social events, but someone not that interested in her when they were alone.

So, the thought of going to that play with her aunt that evening, for curiosity's sake if nothing else, was exciting as she picked out an outfit she hoped would be appropriate for theatre, not to mention if she might meet Bro Gerard.

But even that simple pleasure was to be denied her. Just as the aunt arrived and she was heading out the door, she received a call from Neville, enquiring if she had plans for the evening. When she updated him, he announced that his mother was feeling very unwell. He didn't specifically want Marianne to do anything, but just to be there, in case her condition suddenly worsened. He finished the call by saying he'd be home the following evening and she could go where she liked then. She wanted to scream at him that it would be too late by then but thought better of it.

She made a coffee for Aunt Julie and, as they lamented the non-event of the play, Julie remarked that Marianne seemed unhappy and stressed recently, and that her mother was worried about her. With that, the floodgates opened and she poured everything out to Julie, from her father's passing to Bro Gerard's desertion, to Neville's primary devotion to

84

his mother. It all came out with such a torrent that Julie decided to stay with her that night. Julie also told her that if Neville and she didn't work out, she was welcome to stay with her over the shop.

As Marianne tried to sleep that night, she realised she didn't love Neville at this stage, wondered in fact if she ever had, and tried to figure out how she would end it. It was like she was waiting for something to happen. She was not sure what that something could look like, but when it did happen, it was what she least expected.

As Marianne's emotional struggles were mirroring Charlie's a mere fifty miles from each other, Larry Broderick was announcing the local drama group's plans for the coming season. A full-length play was proposed, and Charlie was asked if he would be interested in writing one.

His first instinct as ever was to have a go, but he would be careful to keep the play theme on safer ground with a softer landing than the previous one.

He wasn't slow to convey this to Vera, who simply said, 'Go ahead. You don't need my permission. You never did, so why start now.'

In this play, which he titled *The Winter of '71*, Charlie decided to work with a theme he was thoroughly familiar with regarding the by now fading practice within certain religious orders in the 1960s and 1970s of recruiting young people of early adolescence age into religious life. Charlie felt that this important piece of Irish History should not be so easily forgotten, that in fact it might be educational from a historical and sociological perspective to the current generation regarding such different times in Ireland not so long ago.

He would cast Larry Broderick as Bro Damien, and even though this play would require quite a large cast, there would be no role for Mary Elizabeth's age. He thought it safer not to include her, and if the child herself noticed, she didn't say. Equally if her mother was happy or unhappy with that, she didn't say. When the play was near completion, he paused to reflect.

Was his memory of that time to be trusted? For he didn't want to wrong anyone in the play but truly wished to write a fair and balanced account of his experiences both good and bad at the time. His biggest questions were as follows. Did that monastery really exist and did Marianne McAndrew really exist? After all, it had been fourteen years since he had been cruelly distanced from both and he was trying to be careful that the actual reality of the facts wouldn't be sacrificed on the altar of his subjective memory, embellished with his love of being creative with the truth.

There was only one way to find out. So Charlie took a day off work and decided to take a nostalgic drive through all the backroads that Digger had taken him through back then, to and from Chapel Hill, thinking it was hard to believe that so many years had lapsed since those days. When they used to arrive at a certain well-known crossroads near his journey's end, from which could be seen the tall spire of that town's church, he remembered how the sight of that spire had always caused a lump to come into his throat, as his father would cheerily say, 'We're nearly there, Digger, nearly there.' But he was brought back into the present as he reminded himself that his mission today was to find out where Marianne McAndrew might now be contacted. He thought the town's Post Office might be a good place to start his enquiries.

The friendly lady at the Post Office seemed very happy to oblige him and told him that Marianne McAndrew was living with a successful agricultural sales manager, Neville St John, a bit outside the town.

She stated loudly, 'I don't believe they ever married, but sure that kind of thing is hardly noticed any more,' as she raised her eyes to heaven and asked him why he wanted to know.

86

On sharing his reason, she became interested and seemed to know a lot about Chapel Hill.

'Big changes up there lately,' she said.

'Oh?'

Charlie suddenly was all ears, which was all the permission the Post Office lady needed to continue.

'Bro James has been moved to one of that Order's houses in India. I believe he'll be no loss,' she whispered as she handed Charlie a slip of paper with Marianne's address on it.

Charlie would have liked to know more about that, but by now a queue was beginning to form behind him, so he thanked her and left. This was precisely why he had come to this town, which boasted the tallest church steeple in Leinster, but once back in his car, a weird feeling came over him.

Was it the news that Marianne was with someone? Had his ego demanded that she would be still waiting for him in a way he didn't for her? Perhaps, he thought. The Post Office lady had said this Neville guy was a successful salesperson. What if she was really happy with him? Would that knowledge disappoint him? Should he leave good enough alone?

As he sat back into his car, the delicious irony of Bro James ending up in India brought a wry smile to his face, which in turn sparked a brainwave. Being so near Chapel Hill, and with Bro James in foreign parts, he felt this strong nostalgic urge to revisit the monastery. Before he had fully thought that brainwave through, he found himself driving up that avenue facing the dark-looking building, the one from the horror movie.

All sorts of memories rushed at him as he approached the big wooden door. He didn't know the young Brother who opened the door to him, so he gave his name and former name as he asked if Bro Damien was still in this house.

The nodding Brother invited him in and, after a few minutes, the wonderful man of God himself came into the waiting room, recognised him, and warmly put his hand out to Charlie.

In a broken voice Bro Damian said, 'Brother Gerard, you were wronged, very wronged.'

Those few words were like gold dust to Charlie, both in that moment and thereafter. He shared tea with Bro Damien, who wanted to know all about his life now and if he had kept up the music playing. He shared about Vera and Mary Elizabeth, for which he was warmly congratulated, and consequently didn't feel it appropriate to mention Marianne McAndrew. But he did tell him about his play based on his time there, and when Bro Damien offered him any help he could and told him to be sure and call again, he said he would like that.

Despite his foreboding about contacting Marianne, the completion of *The Winter of '71* had by now become a really meaningful mission for him and he could not risk continuing without getting his memories confirmed, so he accepted the risk, went into the Post Office and procured writing paper, envelopes and a pen. Sitting in his car, under the shadow of that massive spire, he wrote to Marianne and Neville at the given address. In it he addressed both parties, stating who he was, why he was writing to them after all these years, and about his play which was at the root of his reason for writing. At the end, he said that if he had imagined all of this, or if she had no interest in his project, they could quietly put his letter in the fire. But, just in case his memory was correct or that they might like to help with the project, he shared his work phone number.

…go for it….

A week had passed when the secretary called his work extension a little after 9 o'clock one morning, saying he had missed a call. The caller had left a number, but didn't want to give a name. Charlie recognised the prefix and felt anxious as he dialled the number, hoping it would be her, not Neville, on the other end.

Thankfully, it was Marianne, with her unmistakeable voice unchanged by the passing of time. She still had that energetic tone as she assured him that she did exist back then, she did remember him and wondered where he'd disappeared to all those years ago. In as good a way as a man can do in a phone call, he briefly explained his side of the story and added that he would love the opportunity to meet with her in person and explain more fully where he went then and what he was doing now.

To his surprise, she not only agreed but with a degree of enthusiasm. She said she didn't drive, but there was a bus stop literally outside her door, and there was a special bus on Saturday mornings which would bring her directly to a well-known garden centre not a million miles from her. It had nice walks and a coffee shop, which she hoped would not be too far from him.

Charlie was very definite in his reply. 'Many's a Saturday I would have given my right arm for the chance to meet you again.'

'Let's make it this Saturday in that case,' Marianne replied.

They instantly agreed to meet there for an hour on the following Saturday morning at 10 o'clock.

Charlie's mind raced faster than Larry Broderick's Log Cabin during the following few days. What would she look like now, fourteen years since he last saw her? Would those beautiful eyes look happy or sad? Would it upset him if they were happy? Had he any right to be upset? Would it show? How much of his own story would he share?

Such questions clashed with reality questions like what he would say at home about where he was going. He didn't usually work on Saturdays, so how would he explain his absence, especially to Mary Elizabeth who loved having him home on Saturday mornings? But it was too important, so he devised a reasonably credible work story, which brought disappointment and understanding from the younger party cushioned with a promise to bring something back, while the exact opposite applied from the other. 'You're never here.' But Charlie could live with that.

Two mornings later, Charlie set out to find the nominated garden centre and was happy when he actually got there early. Marianne had given him the number of the bus she would be on, and sure enough, a little bit behind time, he saw it coming. Anxiety crept in when he saw there were a lot of people alighting to enter this seemingly extremely popular garden centre. He was afraid he would either not see or not recognise her. But then he saw her, still tall, still elegant, as beautiful as ever, he waited to see if she would recognise him.

And recognise him she did.

'Where's the collar?' she cheekily asked as she approached him before adding, 'I'm not too sure you're as interesting without it,' quickly followed by, 'What is your real name, anyhow?'

Charlie was happy to share his real name, relieved by her greeting, as they began walking. Some things had not changed in the fourteen years. Marianne still walked as she talked with endless energy, asking him question after question.

'Where do you actually live? Who do you live with?'

But, before he could answer any, her tone changed.

'Why did you run away from me?'

And so their conversation began at a hundred miles per hour, as he told her about the letter he had written her and had posted to her aunt's shop after that night when Bro James had found them by the river. He went on to tell her how disappointed he had been when she hadn't shown up as his letter had requested, and that a week later he had been brought home in disgrace, where he cruelly found out that in fact she never got his letter and why.

Marianne swore she knew absolutely nothing about his letter, neither then or now. To this day, her mother had never told her. She had been told that Bro Gerard could not do the show due him being unwell, and he had been moved to a different monastery, where she assumed he had by choice completely forgotten about her. After fourteen years, the story was beginning to make sense to both parties.

But for Marianne, there were pieces missing from his story.

'If you were able to find me now, why didn't you try to find me back then?'

Charlie continued to defend his position.

'I assumed you had deliberately given my letter to your mother, that I had become some kind of nuisance to you.'

'Never,' she protested. 'I swear I never saw that letter.' He heard Marianne curse under her breath. 'I'll never forgive my mother.'

Charlie, ever the peacemaker, encouraged her not be bitter.

'She did what she felt was the right thing to do at the time, and look, perhaps she was right. Here you are now in a good relationship by the sounds of it.'

But Marianne's anger would not be abated.

'I had a right to see that letter.'

Charlie tried to steer the conversation back to the present.

'Do you have children?' he asked.

'No,' she replied sadly, 'and I'm not exactly in what you could call a good relationship.' She took a deep breath. 'Now, I've said it. It's out there. His name is Neville, a businessman in name but a total mammy's boy by nature.'

Charlie instantly felt bad for feeling so good at hearing the news about the state of her relationship.

'And you?' she asked. 'I see a wedding ring.'

'Yes,' he answered. 'Sadly my marriage to Vera is somewhat like your situation. Vera is a fine lady, but she and I haven't exactly worked out. But we do have a daughter. She's eight and beautiful.'

'What's her name?'

'Mary Elizabeth.'

'Does she look like you?'

'I think the child's very lucky,' he said jokingly. 'She has her mother's good looks but my personality.'

Marianne laughed at that.

'I'm sure that's entirely untrue, Charlie McCann. Now as I hear myself say your name, I love the sound of it.'

He thought he saw relief in her face at his mentioning his own situation, but was it that imagination of his again, the one Bro James wasn't fond of?

'When did you marry?' she asked.

When he shared that it was nine years ago, she sighed and said, 'Imagine, I moved in with Neville about that same time, only fifty miles up the road from you. And neither of us knowing about the other. So sad, don't you think?'

Then, as only Marianne could, she switched gears again.

'Tell me about this play of yours,' she asked, but didn't let him answer before continuing. 'There was a play in a nearby town hall not long ago. *Chains of Freedom* was the name, and I thought it said it was written by you, but I couldn't be sure.'

'And you didn't come to find out?' he asked, acting all disappointed.

In turn, she told him the sorry saga of why she couldn't as he confirmed that it actually was his play.

And so the conversation went, as the agreed hour became two, which became three before either was ready to leave. They had history, but so much in common that when she said she would like if they could meet again, Charlie felt a new sense of being truly alive. And he could always rationalise if not deny such potentially dangerous feelings to himself that it was only research for the new play.

And so it began. The innocent meetings in that garden centre, the easy interesting conversations, updates on the play script, the part her memory played in it, the coffees which became lunches, as respective lives, loves and hobbies were put through the rigours of comparative analysis. They chatted about everything from her place of work to the meaning of life and love, and from the sublime to the ridiculous, music, poetry and films. They were in unanimous agreement on *Ryan's Daughter* being the best fictional movie ever made, even if Marianne wondered how a girl who wanted to become a nun could feel such connection with and sympathy for the lead female character, Rosie Ryan. They also further agreed that the best film based on a true life story, despite its tragic theme, had to be *Sophie's Choice*.

The fact that the former was made in Ireland made it even more special. They enthusiastically, if somewhat naively, agreed that in some time in the future, Charlie would write a stage version of that film and that Marianne would play the title role.

'And you,' she asked, 'will you play the part of Major Doryan?'

'No,' he reflected honestly, 'I think I would be more suited to the boring schoolteacher character, but don't worry. We'll find a Major Doryan for you.'

As Charlie drove home that evening, he felt genuinely like he had back then when they would meet after the concert rehearsals, totally connected. But that is where it remained and would have to stay, so he would have to get used to finding a balance between his life and his heart's promptings. He was married and there was Mary Elizabeth, with whom he was already in trouble for being late. And Marianne was in a relationship, so the illusion of innocence could be sustained. They both had busy lives, so there were no decisions to be made at this point.

When they had been meeting back in the days of Chapel Hill, he knew it to be dangerous, but she didn't seem to care. He now knew the case to be much the same.

One of Marianne's heroes was the poet Pat Ingoldsby, whom she had often come across in Dublin when her aunt was buying from the wholesale merchants there, as he sat selling his books of poems outside the Bank of Ireland. But romance met reality in their most recent meetings, when she excitedly told him she had met Mr Ingoldsby again and had bought his latest book of poems, having gotten Mr Ingoldsby to sign it, *For Charlie, the luckiest man in the whole world.* Before giving the book to him, she read her favourite poem from it called, "Go for It."

It is not possible for you and me to fully explore the waiting glory of you and me without somebody getting hurt. It might be me, it might be you, it might be someone else. But, sure as hell, it's going to be one or more of us. The only way to avoid the hurt is by stopping the unstoppably building tide. The only way to avoid it is by leaving everything and everybody standing still, stuck, exactly where we are. But sure, where is the glory in that?

… a walking contradiction, partly truth and partly fiction…

If Marianne was very enthused about Ingoldsby's poem, Charlie wasn't quite so, especially by her repeated referral to that last line. Yes, it was true that each meeting between them seemed more magical than the one before. They never seemed to run out of things to say, or things to do. But some of her ideas were running a bit too fast for his liking, especially within the theme of that Ingoldsby poem.

For Charlie's world was divided as ever. If being with Marianne was Charlie's romantic zone, his comfort zone was home.

So, when Marianne suggested she would love to come to one of the rehearsals of *The Winter of '71*, his initial excitement at that suggestion had quickly morphed into those same sickening feelings of anxiety. The joy of her interest in something so important to him was jeopardised by the risk of exposure. It was one thing for his local drama group to witness his writing from the safety of past tense. But if they were to witness the past becoming the present before their very eyes, that would be an entirely different proposition. And Charlie knew it.

So he made some weak excuse as to why that might not work. But, later that evening, he cursed himself and his ambiguity on things important. Why couldn't he be one way or the other? He and Vera had recently attended a night out at one of her favourite comedians, in which the comedian told the funny line that if one tries to walk through life with one leg on either side of an electric fence, at some point, the fence will get high. And although the rest of the audience were laughing at that line, Charlie was not and neither was Vera.

Meanwhile, Marianne had become even happier working in the art & craft shop since Charlie's return to her life, as she found herself constantly buying pretty things from the craft shop as presents for Mary Elizabeth, which Charlie decided to give to the child, but claiming he himself had come across them. He felt bad around the lie, but could not deny the child the happiness each little present brought to her smiling face.

But, just like Charlie's not wanting to deny his daughter's happiness, Marianne too no longer wanted to deny herself happiness. Life was short, she thought, thinking of her father. So, on their next meeting, she told Charlie that she was going to tell Neville their relationship was over. She felt it was their time.

If she had imagined that he would be as excited about that as she was, she was rather shocked when he suggested that the timing was not great as far as Mary Elizabeth was concerned.

Marianne assured him that her decision was not designed to put him under any pressure. It was just a decision she felt she needed to make for herself. As Charlie continued to look bothered, it angered her. At that meeting, they had their first row and they both found reasons why they had to go home early. As they were parting, he begged her not to do anything just yet.

Marianne did not sleep that night as she tossed and turned, and on the following morning she had her mind made up to tell Neville the truth. What Charlie had requested of her was unreasonable and unfair, she concluded. So, before Neville left for work, she did tell him. He seemed terribly upset, especially when she told him there was someone else, but didn't say who or where. Neville went quiet and simply said he had to go, would be away overnight and asked if she could hold off doing anything till he got home the following evening. She agreed, but her mind was already made up.

Charlie was her first love and the one she desperately craved to be with. She recognised the part her mother had played in what she perceived as him abandoning her back then, which had reduced her to a state of vulnerability, leading in turn to a rushed relationship with the wrong man. But she was angry that, now that they were being given a second chance, he was again hesitating. She felt determined to plan her next move, with or without Charlie. So she told Aunt Julie, who happily agreed she could move into the room over the shop for now.

But while closing the shop on the following evening, Marianne realised that she was not feeling at all as sure about anything or the planned conversation later with Neville. He had phoned her last night to say he had been doing a lot of thinking over what she'd said, he'd bought her something he knew she would like, he had spoken with his mother about her interference and, from now on, things between them would change.

Why does it always seem, she thought, that men do not seem to know what they have till it's too late. Had Charlie a point? She could hang on another while, perhaps. After all, her impulsivity had been her downfall in the past, and even though she had learned to accept it was part of who she was, nevertheless maybe it was time to learn to rein it in. For now, she would do it Charlie's way, which would no doubt please Neville, which in turn would bring short term ease to herself.

Such thoughts were interrupted by a loud knock on the door.

'We're closed,' she shouted out.

But, through the corner of her eye, she saw Aunt Julie outside with two Gardai, a male and female. She could see that her aunt was looking upset, so she quickly opened the door, which was re-closed just as quickly by her aunt once the Gardai were inside and locked with purpose, as the blinds were drawn.

Marianne froze as Julie looked at her in a shocked state.

'The Gardai want to speak to you privately in the office, Marianne.'

'Can you bring us a pot of tea?' one of the Gardai asked Julie.

Julie immediately addressed their request as they sat Marianne down in the office. The female Garda gently broke the news that Neville had been in a serious car accident.

'How bad?'

'Very bad, I'm afraid.'

'But he'll be ok, won't he?'

In the frozen faces of the two Gardai, she found her answer and quietly began sobbing.

This is déjà vu, she thought, but quickly reframed that to, *I've been here before and I came through it.* And with that, a steely determination came over her.

She calmly thanked the two Gardai and said she would like to be alone with her thoughts for a while. She asked Julie to deal with the Gardai as regards the accident and with Neville's mother about funeral arrangements. When the Gardai said they would need to talk to her again she quietly nodded her agreement. Then, ghost-like, she silently and slowly left the three and returned to the empty closed shop, where she found refuge and a place to reflect.

There she sat quietly in the chair and thought about what she had done the previous morning. Should she tell Julie about that conversation with Neville? Should she tell the Gardai? Was the accident due to his being distracted or tormented or, God forbid, something far worse? She decided to say nothing to anyone for now.

Showing initiative, Julie quietly let the Garda out the back door and left Marianne alone until she was ready.

The following few days were hard, harder than when her father passed away. At least, back then, the guilt belonged to others. Her fight and flight brain was fully engaged throughout, especially when the Gardai interviewed her, as they said they would, and told her there would be an inquest.

'How long will that take?'

'Sadly, we can't say,' was their honest reply.

Were they looking suspiciously at her or was she imagining it? In the few days while she waited for the results of the inquest, she increasingly wanted to come clean. But something held her back.

Eventually Neville's body was released, and the funeral arrangements announced, with her relief that no further questioning from the Gardai was deemed necessary for now, other than informing her that the crash was head-on, on a wide road, involving an articulated truck. Road conditions had been perfect, the Gardai said. This was not what Marianne needed to hear, but she would have to live with it.

She knew that Charlie did not really like being called at work but strongly felt the need to hear at least the comfort of his voice.

When she told him her tragic news, he paused before asking, 'Had you told him about us?'

'Is that all you want to know?' she angrily replied before lying about it, and when he asked if she would like him to attend the funeral, she thought she heard hesitation in his voice and immediately told him it might be best not to. While inside, she felt betrayed, just as Neville perhaps had.

And so, for Marianne, the long week dragged on, from going to see the closed coffin in the funeral home, to the awkward hug with Neville's mother.

Pumping thoughts assailed her constantly. Does she know something? Had he told her about their impending break-up, about this other man? The wake, funeral Mass and burial were each harder than the previous.

Even though Neville's mother was clearly upset, Marianne could almost see the satisfaction in her face that at least her advice to Neville to be slow to marry had paid off. Marianne would have no claim on the house.

Her mother Maria tried to support her, but the deep feeling of betrayal was still there. Where she got unexpected support was from her Uncle Robert, who travelled all the way from Dunstable for the funeral, just as he had for her parents' wedding.

They had a quite chat after the funeral, during which she told him of her situation and he told her his firm had been advertising for an administration manager at his business back in Dunstable and wondered if she might be interested. And he added that the rent-free use of a two-up-two-down house in the centre of Dunstable, which he owned amongst other properties, would come with the position. If she chose to join his firm then 125 West St, Dunstable would be her new address. The salary as far as Marianne was concerned seemed ridiculously high, but if that's how Uncle Robert rated her, why should she devalue herself? She thanked him and promised to think about it.

She approached her next meeting with Charlie with a mixture of sadness, anger and yet longing for him to tell her that everything would be ok and that he would come to Dunstable with her. But when they did meet, it was short and awkward, due to his not offering much comfort over the past few weeks, her lies to him and his indecision about where he and she might go next.

So, partly because of her anger, and partly due to her need to do it, she told him about the offer by her Uncle Robert and how seriously she was considering it. He seemed upset, but not upset enough, she thought, to either talk her out of it or say he'd go with her.

That proved to be the final piece in the move to Dunstable jigsaw for Marianne. For her, the die was cast. Julie understood and thought it a good thing for her to do, adding that her job would remain in the family, that Marianne's mother Maria would step into the breach at the shop, at least short-term, like she had previously.

Marianne had heeded Charlie's counsel re not raising the whole missing letter business with her mother. There seemed little point at this stage. Maria seemed happy for her and added that this was her father Paul's divine intervention to rescue her from a tricky situation and urged her not to think twice about it. But then again, her mother knew nothing of her reconnection with the former Bro Gerard and even less about her daughter's knowledge of the missing letter.

Marianne quickly confirmed to Charlie that she would be leaving for Dunstable as soon as everything was in place. What she did not tell him was that she could no longer remain in the town of the two monasteries, never knowing what somebody might know about Neville's death, or whom he might have spoken to in the thirty hours prior to his accident.

She hated that whole looking over your shoulder feeling and felt that type of guilt could be borne easier in another country than in this valley of the squinting windows, where gossips thrive and facts are scarce.

…don't forget to remember…

Marianne left for Dunstable on October 1st, 1985, and Charlie found himself torn apart once more. Marianne was the kind of woman he should not have to say goodbye to, and now he had done so twice.

At their last arranged meeting, in a quiet cafe before her departure, he had made a cassette tape copy of his favourite music and given it to her, saying, 'Just so that you won't forget me.'

'I think we both know that's unlikely,' she replied.

And that was it. Marianne was gone, again.

As Charlie privately envied what seemed to him to be an easier set of circumstances for Marianne to up and leave than his own, he immediately felt shallow and childish. Were there genuine reasons why he found decisions so difficult, or did he make them difficult? She had reassured him she would like to keep in touch, but she wasn't quite sure about that being the right thing, stating that she genuinely did not want to bring the potential hardship that their relationship held for the child's happiness.

While Marianne was heading into a whole new world, Charlie had the ongoing comfort blanket of home and all that Mary Elizabeth was achieving, becoming an altar server at Mass and joining her school band. Aside from that, he was pleased with how the rehearsals were progressing for *The Winter of '71*.

As regards the situation between Vera and himself, he continued to blame his weakness for going ahead with the marriage despite his doubts, and Vera's potential sixth sense about such doubts. Like Charlie, maybe she too had kept her suspicions to herself, thereby crippling any potential the marriage ever had. But he also knew with great certainty that if Mary Elizabeth had been born to any other mother, she would most definitely not be as special as she was. Vera was a classy lady who turned her daughter out beautifully for all occasions. Their sad situation was nobody's fault. It can just be like that sometimes.

So, as Christmas approached, play rehearsals were in full swing and all was going well. It would go on stage on February 11th for four nights. Charlie was busy organising the usual exciting Christmas build-up for Mary Elizabeth who was still Santa's biggest fan. He decorated the house and pulled out his old Mario Lanza Christmas LP to dust it down in time for Christmas morning. And, if Mary Elizabeth loved the ceremony of it all, it was nothing more than one of his many monastery institutionalised habits, according to her mother.

On December 15th work was really busy before the festive break when the secretary called him.

'There's a letter at reception for you.'

When he saw that the envelope was in Marianne's handwriting, and with an English stamp, he felt a rare combination of fear and that warm glow of anticipation, but decided he would not open it till later. Excitement was one thing, but the contents of the letter might be harder to deal with. For all he knew, she might be telling him she was doing really well in Dunstable and had met someone there. For that reason, he kind of wished she had held off till the New Year. If that was her news, he did not need to be dealing with it now of all times. On second thoughts, he could apply a bit of discipline and hold off reading it until the New Year.

But on Christmas Eve, when Mary Elizabeth and her mother had gone to visit Vera's mother, Charlie's curiosity got the better of him and he opened the letter.

Hello Charlie,
I hope all is ok with you. I am doing ok, if homesick. I really like my job and am doing good there. I love my home in the middle of a crazy busy street.

But I will not lie. I miss you, Charlie, and wish I felt as brave now as I did at our last meeting, but I don't. I've been thinking about you a lot, especially with the season that's in it, and knowing your play rehearsals must be getting to an exciting stage by now.

I know of your responsibilities, so I know I should not really be telling you this, but I can't help how I feel and want to share it with you. Equally, I know I shouldn't offer this, but I'm wondering if, sometime in the New Year, you'd like to come visit me, just for a few hours even. Between the airport, flying etc, I know it would be a long day for you, and I know you do not like being away from Mary Elizabeth, so I'll fully respect whatever decision you make, but I so hope to see you again, even if only for a few hours.

I would love to hear from you. But I will understand if you'd prefer not to. More in hope than expectation, I include my contact details.
Marianne x

The contents, while not containing his biggest fear, still managed to disturb Charlie. As ever a man of contradictions, in some ways this was what he was hoping to hear, but he fully realised that he had been a willing party to the lonely and alone situation in which Marianne now found herself and that he, if nothing else, was not lonely.

The timing of this letter was not good, just as the timing of her moving to Dunstable was not good. Would the timing ever be good, and if not, why had he become involved with her to such a degree? But he did have an eight-year-old in the house for Christmas and could not be distracted by her letter, so Charlie did what Charlie does. He kicked the proverbial can down the road.

He simply returned a Christmas postcard that acknowledged her letter, saying he would be in touch in the New Year. But as he posted it, he wondered why he was acting so coldly. Was it that, deep down, he believed she had deliberately gone ahead and told Neville about them to put pressure back on him before Neville's accident? If so, that would be a heavy burden for him to carry.

Secure in that doubt, and in the comfort of the self-righteousness of doing the right thing by his family and extended family at Christmas, he convinced himself that his action was the correct one. He further convinced himself that once the Christmas loneliness period was behind her, Marianne would find her way, and it would not be too long before she did meet someone else, someone not shackled with as many responsibilities and consequential guilt as he had. Maybe that would be best for all.

And indeed Charlie's Christmas was really good.

But the magic which this time of year promised quickly faded into an extremely stormy February. The play rehearsals helped through this limbo period, and the performances themselves were an enormous success, not alone in his home village hall, but equally when they took it to a nearby city's theatre.

But that too was just another honeymoon period, positive newspaper reviews etc, which quickly evaporated into winter's reality once more, in more ways than one.

And by the time St Patrick's Day came around, the afterglow of the play had definitely regressed into the old familiar relationship fault-lines within his marriage. With each passing day, the temptation to take Marianne up on that one-day-visit offer came back into his tormented mind.

St Patrick's Day morning was unbelievably bad, beginning with their abandonment of a planned family trip to one of the local town parades which Mary Elizabeth loved. Vera suddenly didn't feel up to it at the last minute, having dressed the child beautifully for the occasion.

Charlie decided to split logs outside to regulate his frustration as much as the need for firewood. And, as ever, it was not long till the child excitedly came to help. They were busy with their particular task when an angry Vera shouted out at them from the door.

'Why did you not change her clothes? They're ruined now!'

She called the upset child indoors, leaving Charlie with those familiar feelings that he could do nothing right, as he kept on chopping wood.

But the lovely memory of his little daughter happily helping him a few brief moments ago quickly morphed into the nightmare sounds of a bitterly crying child emanating from inside the house, before turning into screams.

Something deep within Charlie snapped as he dropped the hatchet and ran into the house faster than he had ever previously done. Vera had taken off all the child's good clothes which were lying on the kitchen floor alongside the washing machine. The sight of this and of her furiously scrubbing the child's hands and face at the kitchen sink was too much for him.

'For God's sake, will you leave that poor misfortunate child alone. Her being happy is surely far more important than how fucking clean she or her clothes are!'

The look of thunder on Charlie's face made Vera stop her cleaning, just as the sound of his own raised voice had equally made him retreat.

Charlie ran back out as quickly as he had come in and continued to exercise his anger on the blocks, as he swore out loud to himself. 'This situation is neither right nor is it safe any longer. The poor child can't be listening to this every day. And if it's not right for me, it can't be right for the child.'

That incident was sufficient in itself to reactivate his longed-for trip to Dunstable.

He called into a travel agent the next day and checked flights. With this information to hand, he called Marianne that very evening, offering her various windows. She sounded happy to hear from him and immediately accepted

106

one of those windows. Charlie booked his ticket on the following day.

… no matter what they call us, however they attack; no matter where they take us, we'll find our own way back …

It was a miserable April morning in 1986 as Charlie set off for Dublin Airport, having tossed and turned the previous night.

But by the time he arrived at Dublin Airport and parked, thankfully the weather was kinder, the sun had come out and he felt better. He had never seen the inside of a plane previously, so was excited if anxious as he made his way through the airport and identified the correct gate for the flight to Luton. The fact that he had zero luggage helped.

And when the time came for him to board, he was pleasantly surprised at how natural it all seemed to be. The stewardess who greeted him entering the plane helped to relax him even more. So, by the time he sat himself down in his window seat, his earlier anxiety turned effortlessly into excitement at the thought of seeing Marianne. Within the safety of this metal bird and the paradoxical freedom it represented, his monastery collar loosened to the point where he began to feel an unreal sense of calm as the hum of conversation and the soft background music helped.

He recognised unexpected feelings of being carefree again as he glanced around the plane like an excited schoolboy. There were couples chatting about wherever they were going, while others like himself were silent solo travellers. He put his hand in his inside pocket to ensure the bracelet he had purchased for Marianne the previous day was still there in its beautiful wrapping. Then the engines roared and the plane was speeding down the runway, a feeling he had absolutely not been looking forward to, but suddenly it all became part of this magical excursion as the plane took off, letting go of his fears as it did so. He gazed out the window at the city shrinking below, as the buildings became like little dots and the landscape transformed into a patchwork of fields and roads. And when the sign said to remove his belt, he felt he was absolutely floating on air, far above the clouds of his struggles.

Sadly all too soon, the captain was speaking to them again to announce they would be landing, but that high was replaced with anticipation as he arrived at Luton Airport and excitedly began to visualise what seeing Marianne again would be like.

And when he saw her standing smiling, he knew he had made the correct decision to come, as they held each other and kissed as if their lives depended on it.

And when they got inside 125 West St and he gave her the present, she immediately said, 'I'll open it later,' as she took him upstairs.

She had arranged it so they would have the day to themselves. He loved her house. The music tape he had given her when she was coming over was playing as he entered and being with her there was everything for which he had hoped. She had prepared his favourite simple kind of food and, as they sat together for hours later watching a video recording of *Ryan's Daughter* which she had managed to procure specially for the occasion, he knew exactly what was missing in his marriage.

As Charlie said goodbye to Marianne that evening, he told her he truly loved her and would find a way to be with her. She acknowledged his love as she returned it and he knew he had never before experienced complete feelings like these for anyone else ever. Marianne's interest in Mary Elizabeth seemed as genuine as it was comforting. A way would have to be found where all three could be permanently together, but Marianne, despite the romantic picture being proposed and her liking of his child, gently reminded both of them both of the possible difficulties associated with that. But in that perfect moment, Charlie wasn't really listening.

…something inside has died…

After that one-day visit to Dunstable, the space in his heart and endorphin-brain for Marianne expanded and the picture of them being together became something that could no longer be ignored. But, to complicate matters for Charlie, Vera happily shared with him on his return that she had been back to her doctor after the St Patrick's Day incident and had agreed to take medication for what had been diagnosed as generalised anxiety.

She could already feel the pills were making a difference.

And, in the weeks that followed, the evidence at home suggested that. She seemed to have more positivity and was more cheerful and loving towards Mary Elizabeth.

This was something Charlie had longed for all his married life, but, having virtually given up on it, had not bargained for it to happen at this particular juncture. Something inside had died, so when she showed renewed interest in their intimate life, he struggled, through a combination of guilt and anger, but again adopted a strategic approach. This triggered the Charlie of old, the one who was heartbroken going to Chapel Hill, and heartbroken leaving it. It seemed nothing could ever be simple.

Charlie did know one thing. He was still going nowhere without Mary Elizabeth. But how could bringing her with him be emotionally, logistically, or legally possible? Not to mention the chronic anticipatory guilt which by now was interfering with his sleep. He became very much aware that his stated reason for bringing the child with him no longer really existed, so Vera wondered why her good news didn't seem to be welcomed as much by Charlie as she had hoped.

Not for the first time, Vera had little idea of the silent conversation that was going on in Charlie's head precisely at that moment. Why could she not have gone to the doctor as he'd suggested years ago? Why had she been so stubborn? And why did she choose now of all times to do it? He continued to rationalise what was now for him a done deal of being with Marianne. *It's a bit too late for our marriage at this late stage and it probably won't last, like all such previous attempts at a quick fix.* But if he could quell his conscious mind with logic, his unconscious was something quite different.

In one of his disturbing dreams, he was on the jury of a courtroom drama and was listening intently to the case for the prosecution.

'What the defendant is thinking of doing is madness. How will his nine-year-old child cope with such disruption to her young life? How will his aging parents cope with his decision? How can he even consider doing this to them, keeping in mind the deep connection between them and their doting granddaughter? For the last five or so years of the child's life, after walking the short distance from school to them each weekday, she gets her dinner, while they help as much as they can with her homework and engage in playful exercises with her until he collects her. The thought of separating the child from this, her second home, is surely outlandish, not to mention the whole impact on the child's mother.'

In direct comparison, the dream's case for the defence seemed weak and flawed.

'His parents have had their life and seemed to have real love in their lives, and surely he is entitled to the same. Marianne, Mary Elizabeth and he would find a way, and in time Vera would get over it.'

He woke from that particular dream in a cold sweat, with a retriggering of that disturbing image of his mother's tear-filled face through the rear window of Digger's car when he was leaving home for the monastery all those years earlier, imprinted on his brain. That picture would certainly be recreated for Maggie. Not alone would her possibly favourite son be gone from her life again, but this time bringing her beloved granddaughter with him. And, with more time on their hands in the years since Marty started taking on more of the farm work, Martin had grown really fond of his granddaughter and she of him.

Charlie knew the case was weak and, if his dream was based on reality, as a jury member he would wonder how the case ever even got to court, never mind succeed.

But such doubts were by now but a mild irritation. The runaway train had already left the station, with 125 West St its final destination.

He had posted a letter to Vera the day before the carrying out of the plan, saying that the child was safely with him but leaving no forwarding address. He knew the postman didn't reach his house till late afternoon any day, by which time they would be gone.

… only a winter's tale…

If his research play *Chains of Freedom* had ended in a dream with no one upset, hurt or damaged, this was most certainly not the case now. In fact it was the ultimate proof of the vast gulf between stage and life. Charlie's Dunstable dream was fraught with problems and his homecoming from Dunstable was always going to be, as his Aunt Maureen might have said, *anything but good*.

As he returned alone through Dublin Airport on 30th June 1986 and noticed the toilets, his mind instantly skipped back to May 1st and his sheer panic at Mary Elizabeth's urgently asking him to bring her to the toilet as they were about to board, but not wanting to go in on her own. Charlie had no idea as to what the protocol for such a situation might be. Luckily a female airport security guard agreed to accompany the child, which thankfully sorted that particular problem.

This was to be the first of many such challenges. Were these red flag warnings that the whole idea was doomed to failure and that he himself was a failure in ever thinking that the complex web of deceit he had created with his innocent daughter could have worked? The plan had been highly idealistic, and he could not understand why he had not remembered the wise words of the poet T.S. Eliot about separating the Idea and the Reality.

His brother Marty was waiting for him at the Arrivals hall, and when Charlie spotted him, strangely, considering the state of his frazzled mind at the time, he noticed that the Abbaesque hairstyle of the dashing young Marty had morphed into a bald but still handsome man, a few inches short of Charlie in height.

Marty's home would be Charlie's home for the present time. The two brothers chatted long into the night about all that had happened since he had left.

'I don't have children, Charlie,' Marty said, 'so I'm no expert on such matters. But I do know you and Vera weren't happy for a very long time, and it was obvious to a blind man how close you are to the child, so I've been defending you.'

'That means a huge amount,' Charlie replied.

'I haven't always been the best big brother, to be honest,' Marty continued, 'and I often thought you were a bit soft, especially when you went into that monastery.'

'That's ok,' Charlie said. 'I often thought myself that I was a bit soft.'

'What happened over there in the snatching back of the child wasn't right. I'm not one bit happy about it.'

'I know, and don't think I don't appreciate you saying that, Marty, but if I'm to have any hope of being with Mary Elizabeth again, I'll have to let that drop.'

But Marty wasn't promising anything yet.

'Can I presume you know who organised it?'

Charlie didn't answer, which Marty understood, but he continued.

'You told me before that Vera had some in-laws up North who had some paramilitary background, isn't that right? Was it them, do you think?'

Charlie gave a pleading look.

'It's ok. I do understand what's at stake for you now. But I can tell you one thing. They shouldn't get away with it. You shouldn't let them away with it!' Marty said in a raised voice. 'But you know what's best, Charlie.'

He did however give Charlie some advice regarding the local gossip.

'If you drink, you're a fool. If you don't, you're a miser.'

But when Charlie awoke the following morning, in yet another strange bed in yet another strange room, his head was sore and his heart sorer. He wondered how Marianne had spent the night as he equally wondered how he would be able to live with her total absence from his life and his plans.

As he worried about how he could ever integrate himself back into his local village life, he wondered how Mary Elizabeth's mother might greet him and if she would ever again trust him.

Marty thought a quick visit to his father and mother might be a good place to start.

And so, on the following morning, Charlie and Marty travelled together to meet them. The scene was reminiscent in ways of his arrival home from the monastery fifteen years previously, same house, same parents, same bothered Charlie, but no Uncle Jack, who had sadly passed away between then and now.

Thankfully, his mother was now as she had been then, showing unconditional love at its best. His father was also similar as back then, initially silent and seemingly disapproving before changing to a more conciliatory stance.

Charlie was relieved that his parents had accepted him home, but he was conscious they made zero mention of "the other woman" as they carefully walked the fine line between not condemning while not condoning his actions. Their acceptance of him being back would for now be sufficient in itself. And if there had been no judgement or questioning of his actions in that encounter, Charlie did not expect any such good fortune from here on in. As far the village were concerned, they probably had dismissed his little trip through the lens of one of Charlie's flights of fancy.

The sympathy of the village lay firmly in Vera's corner and Charlie could understand that. So it was on that understanding that he had made a phone call to Ailish earlier that morning from his brother's phone, seeking to meet Vera or her sister at his brother's house on an evening that would suit them to talk about the possibility of access to Mary Elizabeth.

Ailish said she would meet him alone. His brother Marty, while conscious of his promise to Charlie, still did not feel sure he could keep quiet, so he said it would be better for him to head off on his bicycle and leave the two of them at it.

She arrived that evening at six o'clock, with a resting face that spoke volumes, and a tone to match.

'How is Vera?' was Charlie's tentative opening.

'She doesn't want your name even mentioned in your own house. Does not that say it all?'

What Ailish didn't say to him after that wasn't worth saying as he remained silent, even after she'd finished, trying hard to be a good disciple of Kipling. But if that was meant to impress this particular lady, it didn't work.

'Have you nothing to say for yourself? There's something not right with you. I told Vera you need to see a psychiatrist before she lets you near Mary Elizabeth again.'

At that moment, Marty, who had apparently heard the last sentence, walked in.

'And I suppose there is everything right in organising a bunch of ex-paramilitaries wearing balaclavas to snatch an innocent child?'

'That is none of your business,' Ailish snapped back at him, as Charlie kept shaking his head towards his brother in a pleading fashion, 'and for your brother's sake, don't make it your business. And I would strongly advise you now to presume nothing and say nothing about anything to do with that morning in Dunstable.'

With that, she turned on her heel. Her car sent stones flying in the driveway as she drove out the gate.

…if I can forget her and not let it show…

Two weeks back in his native village and Charlie was experiencing something not dissimilar to his return from the monastery fifteen years previously. People from the village did not know or care in either case as to why he went or what he left behind him to return.

He knew how locals could talk, and according to his mother they had, and he could see the awkwardness in the local shops whenever he entered. And when he risked attending Mass alone, he could see heads turning. It was particularly in those situations that he found his brother's gem of wisdom regarding gossip useful.

So this was far from the perfect time for a meeting with Vera, but she had requested to meet him, so he could not avoid it. This meeting would be the first time seeing her since he left home that morning over two months ago.

His brother had again vacated his home. Vera certainly didn't feel up to seeing Charlie yet, but Mary Elizabeth had continued to ask about her father, so she knew she could no longer put off agreeing to some kind of plan. Her sister would drive her to the brother's house and would remain in the car. Marty would burn off his anger on his bike once more, having promised Charlie there would be no early return.

The sisters were late and, by the time they arrived, the chatter inside Charlie's head and heart was like a raging furnace. Here was the ultimate face-the-music moment and he was not one bit ready, so much so that the narrative he had composed for the occasion completely deserted him.

As he watched her getting out of the car, he instantly noticed that she had lost a considerable amount of weight, and her face looked ashen and drained of blood.

But as he opened the door, and she was standing there, all he could ridiculously think of saying was, 'You look well.'

'Another lie, Charlie. I see nothing has changed. If you have any ambitions of seeing my daughter again, I will insist that you see a psychiatrist.'

'You mean *our* daughter.'

'No man who did what you have done to that poor child deserves to be called her father.'

He tried to fumble a response.

'I know it can't have been easy for you.'

'How would you know? You weren't here. You were busy, shall we say, in other areas.'

Charlie didn't reply.

'I presume you believed that she and you were a match made in heaven.'

Charlie hesitated. 'No relationship is perfect.'

'But obviously you felt it was perfect enough to ruin my life and that of Mary Elizabeth, and for what? Just to be with her?'

He was now struggling, knowing every answer he gave might make the difference between seeing his daughter again or not.

'It was a mistake.'

'A mistake. Ah, so that's all it was. And there was I foolishly thinking in other terms, like adultery, or betrayal, or child abduction.'

Charlie was dying to say something about leaving child abduction to the experts in her corner, but caught in this walking-on-thin-ice conversation, and in the interest of damage limitation, Charlie decided yet again that a strategic approach would be best.

'Ok, maybe it was more than a mistake, but *she* was a mistake.'

'You chose her not alone to be your new life partner but also to be *my* child's mother. She did her best, and all you can say about her is that she was a mistake. I presume you gave her the same line about me to get her into bed.'

Vera had obviously been bottling this up and it had festered.

'As long as I live, I will never forgive you for what you have done. After this, how can I ever possibly believe you again about anything?'

She took a good look around at Marty's house.

'I hope you've settled here, because here is where you'll be staying.'

As she turned towards the door, Charlie felt a sense of relief that it was over. But he had to risk the question that was foremost on is mind.

'How is Mary Elizabeth?'

'I know that she's the only reason you came back and that she's the only reason you agreed to meet me. She's happily back in her own bed, her own school and with her own friends, and you'll never get the chance to take that away from her ever again.'

Charlie nodded in agreement for, in the cold light of day, he had accepted that no one has the right to take that kind of security away from an innocent child, not even him.

'What about my seeing her?'

'That will be up to her and others, for I'm not the only one who has doubts about you, Charlie, after this whole sorry saga. Go see that psychiatrist!'

And with that, she was back in her sister's car and he was alone, with her words ringing in his ear and Marianne keeping her no contact part of the bargain. Charlie took time out to assess the situation as he accepted there had been no winners in any of this whole sorry business.

…how do you mend a broken heart…

As a broken hearted Marianne continued to struggle a month after Charlie's desertion of her, she thought of a line that Sister Teresa had often quoted in class. *We don't always have to make life happen; sometimes it just happens to us.* She figured that life was unlikely to happen to her while cooped up in her house feeling sorry for herself, so on Saturday mornings she began walking from her house and ending up back there, increasing the walk from week to week. "Enjoying" might be a stretch too far, but at least she was getting out and avoiding that awful feeling of loneliness.

It was while on one of those Saturday morning walks that a Jaguar XJ12 pulled up alongside her and she heard a 'Hello,' which she chose to ignore, even if the accent was quite distinct and interesting.

'I'm looking for directions,' he said. 'I'm sorry if I startled you,' and he started to drive off again.

She thought for a second, before having a quick change of heart.

'I'm meeting someone,' she called out, 'but maybe I can help you.'

He stopped the car again.

'I appreciate that. I'm looking for the nearby Catholic church. There's a funeral there in ten minutes that I need to get to.'

Marianne knew the church he was looking for was quite close as she had often noticed it, if never actually getting around to going in.

'I can try to direct you, but you'll probably never find it,' she said.

'Don't suppose you'd care to hop in and show me, please?'

Whether it was the adrenalin of the walk or sheer lack of adult company, Marianne found herself in the passenger seat of the luxurious car and they were making their way towards the church.

He laughed. 'Thought you were meeting someone.'

With her directions, he quickly found the church and thanked her. Before she got out, she asked who the funeral mass was for.

'For my ex-wife, so this might be awkward,' he said as he held the door open for her. 'Thanks again. My name's Ricki.'

Marianne resumed her walk and was quite shocked at the impact this brief interlude with a total stranger could have on her.

But in an instant cloudburst, as the heavens opened the minute he went into the church and she not having a raincoat, that brief dream washed away, and was just as quickly replaced by feelings of self-ridicule for even entertaining such thoughts. *Will I ever learn?* she thought as, not for the first time, she cursed her foolish imagination.

Two weeks later, Marianne awoke early, feeling deeply troubled. This morning represented a couple of major milestones. Six weeks to the day had elapsed since Charlie's departure, and today was her father's twenty-fifth anniversary. Her mother had written to her weeks previously, inviting her home for the anniversary Mass.

But Marianne's anger with her mother had not abated. If Bro Gerard's letter had been rightly handed over to the person whose name was on the envelope, her first love and she might have had a hope, however slim, of ending up together. But by the time they had found each other again, too much had happened for their chances of getting together having any real hope. So no, she would not be going home for her father's anniversary Mass.

But I can't stay stuck here either, she thought. Needless to remark, the Jaguar driver had not crossed her path again, and she felt stupid for ever thinking he would.

She was so lonely at times that she had often thought about returning to Ireland, but instinctively felt that would only make things worse for everyone, for she knew there would be expectations of her doing just that. She continued to give herself a tough time for her ultimatum to Charlie about no further contact. It made sense at the time, but now she was not so sure if in fact anything she had done at the time made much sense.

The one bright spot in her life was, despite everything, she was still incredibly happy in her job. McAndrew Construction was situated in the largest unit of a recently built industrial estate on the outskirts of Dunstable. Robert was owner, Project Director and Managing Director. Like all such firms, there was a host of sections within the unit: sales & marketing, design, project management, design management, engineering, quantity surveying, accounting etc. Marianne worked in the HR department and her specific role was to be a link person between all the other departments to ensure good customer relations, smooth communication, deliveries on schedule etc. She was good at her job, popular in the workplace and there had been that recent chat with Uncle Robert about maybe it being time for her to move up the management chain.

In her idle moments, her romantic brain could fantasise that the universe might decree she and Charlie might meet again, sometime, somewhere. But she equally knew why that would not be happening anytime soon. For if Charlie were to have any chance of playing a meaningful role in Mary Elizabeth's life, something so important to him that he had chosen to end their relationship, he would have to try to restore trust.

Marianne concluded that, in this world of uncertainty, the only certainty was that she would have to get used to her life just as it was. But as she sat thinking about all of this, she felt guilty for not honouring her father's landmark anniversary in some form. She was stuck, not being able to see a way forward, which reminded her of Charlie's state of stuckness when his child had been taken.

She knew that she could not allow that stuckness to develop in the way it had in Charlie, so she pushed herself to get up, shower and get dressed. She would walk to the local church and light a candle for her father.

Even the thought of that made her feel better, as did the walk itself, despite the likeness between the grey morning and her mood. As she approached the church, the first thing that struck her was the choir music. It was beautiful but sad and she wondered what had happened to the spirited young woman of years ago who had loved fun, loved singing, who had loved life.

Where had that girl gone? Those were her thoughts as she entered the church. Mass was on, again raising memories of a life lost somewhere. Possibly because she was a stranger, or probably because Mass was over and everyone was turning to leave, she felt every head turn to see who the intruder was. Luckily, there was one vacant seat in the back pew and she was happy to render herself invisible as she sat there. She maintained this invisibility status when the Mass ended, as the church quickly emptied apart from a few souls who remained back to light candles for loved ones, which was her cue.

But she would wait just a little longer. This was something she wanted to do in a private moment between herself and her beloved father. And when that moment finally arrived, or so she thought as she approached the candelabra, a gentleman from the choir came down the stairs from the choir gallery and looked around before speaking to her.

'Just to say we're going to practice a few new hymns now, so we hope we're not disturbing you.'

She assured him that the distraction would be welcome, which seemed not to go unnoticed by him.

'Would you care to join us? We're always looking for new members.'

'You are truly kind,' she replied, 'but work away. I'm only lighting a few candles for someone and then I'll leave you to your singing.'

'Forgive me, but would you mind if I asked who the candles are for?'

Normally such an intrusion would not be welcomed by Marianne, but he seemed such a caring man that she found herself telling him about her father and his early passing.

'You seem like such a lovely lady,' he said. 'I'm sure your father would be very proud of you.'

She did not feel worthy of such an accolade, but welcomed it. But that gentleman was not quite finished.

'But you're also perhaps a very lonely lady. If you change your mind, pop up to us when you have your business here done.'

With that, the gentleman disappeared back to his choir colleagues and she lit her candles.

When she had that task complete, she looked out the church door at the grey headstones and the emptiness of the grey Sunday late morning over the lonely town, just as the choir had begun rehearsing their new hymn. What would she be going back to her house for? There was nothing to do there, only wait for work on Monday morning.

Without her realising it, she found herself walking up those stairs. Two hours later, as she walked down the same stairs, for the first time in a long time, she had discovered a brief respite from loneliness and a sense of belonging again. It seemed that Sister Teresa might have had a point after all.

124

...to everything, turn, turn, turn...

Back in Ireland, to honour Vera's non-negotiable condition, Charlie sought a referral from his local doctor to a psychiatrist, who wrote a report after meeting him twice and sent it back to the doctor, who in turn had given it to Charlie, who gave it to Vera.

He must have passed, for, not long after, Ailish called him to say that she had been appointed by Vera to facilitate access with Mary Elizabeth, saying that Vera didn't want anything to do with it.

Initially, the conversation between Charlie and his daughter seemed awkward, or was that Charlie's projection again? But as time passed, so did the awkwardness.

Charlie wanted to know if she was ok after the four weeks away from home and school, but all Mary Elizabeth would say was, 'I'm home now.'

Luckily, his job at the local Co-op had remained unfilled, so Mr Broderick welcomed him back without any explanation. And, little by little, Charlie got back busy in work and in life.

But more changes were afoot. Marty had met a lady, some months previously, who he only ever referred to as *that woman I know from Clonmel,* and he awkwardly said that she'd like to maybe come see where he lived some evening. Charlie was beginning to feel a bit in the way, without being told as such.

Quietly, a plan was agreed with his parents that he would move back into his childhood home, telling Marty that he wanted to be closer to Mary Elizabeth, and there was an element of truth in that. It meant that, after school, the child would get a lift to her grandparents, where they would get to spend precious time with her before Charlie's coming home from work.

She would then go home for her dinner, while Charlie would sit at the dinner table with his parents, a case of going back to the future. But such was Charlie's new life, while the village gossips had thankfully found other poor carcasses to feast upon. Mary Elizabeth loved being back home, her friends and her school. That was enough for Charlie, who continued to settle and struggle in equal measure.

On the one hand, he could consider himself blessed to be part of Mary Elizabeth's life again, his parents' lives, and life within the local community. But he was looking for some kind of a change to his life, something to give it more meaning, as he rambled into his local shop after work one evening, picked up a newspaper and looked at the opportunities page.

Whether it was fate or providence or both, one advertisement stood out to him.

Have you ever considered a career in counselling? We are a newly-established private college, offering opportunities to mature students to train as therapists, currently not available to mature students. Why not contact us with a view to undertaking a part-time accessible and affordable Foundation programme with us.

When he called the number the following morning, he found the receptionist helpful. What he would be looking at initially, she explained, was a six month part-time foundation programme. Once successfully completed, it would serve as a second-chance opportunity gateway to a degree for someone like him who, for whatever reason, had not been able to access college education up to this point. This seemed made for him.

The appropriate literature arrived the following day, and he could see that the course, its ethos and its rationale seemed tailor-made. At this stage of his life, aged thirty-four, he was in the last-chance saloon as regards a proper career and so he requested an application form, which duly

126

arrived. As he anxiously scanned through it, there did not seem to be any major roadblocks in the actual form, but he became anxious that a required interview would expose some of his Achilles heels and idiosyncrasies. Such anxieties could wait for now.

The completed form was blessed with Knock Holy Water, a present from his Aunt Maureen. In doing this, he realised that his faith was somewhat of an a la carte nature, but he was desperate.

Whether or not it was due to the holy water, he was delighted to be offered an interview in the Dublin HQ of the college one week later. When he arrived, all suited and booted, he was shown into a large room in which twenty or so other hopefuls had gathered. Tea, coffee and nervous chat flowed for the next fifteen minutes or so, until a tall gentleman by the name of Liam was introduced as one of the college founder members. An impressive, warm and confident-looking man in his mid-fifties, bearing a charismatic presence, Liam effortlessly quoted from many of the founders of principles of counselling, one of which in particular made quite the impression on Charlie.

'When you look at the studies on what makes for effective therapy,' Liam began, 'it's not the technique of the therapist. Neither is it their formal academic qualifications nor the insights of the therapist that made the difference. Rather it's the capacity of the therapist to actually offer the client safety, confidentially and freedom from judgement or shame, combined with active listening skills, as they offer their clients a free and uncontaminated space wherein they were encouraged and supported to see and hear themselves perhaps for the first time.'

He effortlessly paraphrased Ernest Hemingway. 'In our darkest moments, we don't need advice. What we truly need is the power of human connection; a quiet presence, the smallest gesture that indicates we are not alone. Such a warm connection becomes the anchor that holds us steady when life feels overwhelming.'

To embellish the point, he offered an easy to understand metaphor which perfectly reflected the above.

'A good listener is like a talented keyboard player at a cabaret or a wedding. As is often the case in such joyous occasions, someone from the audience can be volunteered to sing. The unexpected singer might not know the precise name of this favourite song, or the key they sing in. The good keyboard player smiles at this and gently encourages them to start wherever they're comfortable in their own time. Before the singer gets to the second line of the song, the keyboard player instinctively and effortlessly uses his musical ear to tune in at precisely the right key. And should the singer change key ten times during the song, they continue to be equally accompanied in whatever key they may have meandered into.' He concluded with, 'The musician has a talent, a patient musical ear. Therapists offer the same, without the keyboard.'

As Charlie listened spellbound, Liam further cemented the valuable lesson by explaining that the opposite to such a person-centred, patient and skilled accompanist would be equivalent to a karaoke machine, which played the computer-programmed melody with no allowance for human imperfections, thereby not alone turning a deaf ear to the singer, but in fact shaming them and exposing their vulnerabilities. He concluded that piece by stating that the first ethical responsibility of therapists is to *do no harm*.

Little could Charlie have known at that moment that not alone was he in the presence of this greatest teacher, but he was equally experiencing a crucial moment in what would turn out to be one of the most positive introductions and experiences of his life, an experience from which he thankfully would never look back.

His scheduled one-to-one interview followed, facilitated by Liam and the other co-founder of the college. He had become conscious during the group discussion that there was a lot of academia amongst his fellow applicants; teachers, nurses, some with degrees in psychology, psychiatric nurses, and a social worker. And here he was, a salesperson, trying to compete with those learned people for a limited number of places on the course.

He decided that honesty was the only policy, so in his one-to-one interview he was just that, honest to a fault.

On his way home, he felt he had done all he could do. It was now in the lap of the Gods. He had deliberately not told anyone about this latest venture. He knew he could manage disappointment himself, but he had a strong feeling that those who cared for him were perhaps tired of supporting him, so he wouldn't put them through that again. If he were offered a place on the foundation course, that would be time enough to tell them. But of course when the letter came, he could feel his anxiety rising as he opened it.

The follow-up letter neither confirmed his place on the course nor excluded him. It simply thanked him for his attendance and said that they would like to meet with him again. Sounds like a second interview, he thought, with a certain trepidation.

…hello again; hello…

In Dunstable, Marianne's life had taken a bit of a turn for the better. In the few weeks since she had joined the church choir, not alone had she made friends but she also rediscovered a big part of her former self. And that gentleman who had spoken so kindly to her in the church on her visit that Sunday turned out to be an unattached gentleman named Archie, older than her, but someone who's company, attention and conversation she really enjoyed.

He seemed intensely interested in everything about her, her history, her break-up with Charlie, and about her job.

Having established that Archie was seemingly happily unattached, stating that he had become too fond of his own company and that no one could live with him, Marianne's mind was at ease. He seemed to some extent to be similar in personality and thinking to Charlie, sufficiently so to cause sadness initially. And, as Charlie and herself once became intrigued at the closeness of their surnames (McCann v McAndrew), she now couldn't help but notice the first name spelling overlap between Archie and Charlie. What way does my mind work at all, she wondered.

A rather sophisticated gentleman, Archie's motto in life was to never speak without thinking and to never think without reading. Little by little, he became an important figure in her life, and she in his, and when they were asked to share a duet for one particular hymn in the choir, both the hymn "Whispering Hope" and the coincidence of the duet felt like déjà vu from somewhere a long time ago.

But she was equally beginning to enjoy her time alone much more than had been the case. It was on one of those times alone, on a Saturday morning routine walk, that the same Jaguar pulled up alongside her again.

'I promise, I'm not stalking you,' the same driver said.

'I didn't think you were,' she replied, with an *I don't care* attitude she wasn't feeling.

'Apologies for my presumption.'

'Apology accepted. Could it be your ex-wife's remembrance Mass already?'

'Sorry?'

'Your ex-wife's funeral Mass, remember?'

'Oh that. No, not yet.' He laughed.

She wondered why he found such a sad reminder to be a source of humour.

'As it happens,' he said, 'this morning I'm also looking for directions, to a café. I'm due to meet someone there.'

Marianne could not help herself.

'You really don't know this area at all, do you?'

He didn't seem to find her observation amusing, but put her on the spot instead.

'Will you have breakfast with me?'

Marianne hesitated. 'I thought you were meeting someone?'

'Yes, and I would like them to meet you.'

Marianne's interest and ego were equally aroused and within seconds she found herself being driven to the café he was looking for, one which she knew extremely well, for Charlie, Mary Elizabeth and herself would have gone there on the occasional Saturday morning. So she wondered why of all places, he had chosen there.

But, acting like a gentleman, he dropped her at the front door as he went to park. While she waited, she felt sadness at the memories and wondered why this guy might be driving around this area which he didn't seem to know, looking for a pretty well-known café.

He came to rejoin her from inside, which she thought odd. As he held the café door open for her, he said, 'Hope you remembered my name.'

'How could I forget. I had a teacher called Ricki once. Mind you, he was nothing like you.' Marianne smiled as she looked around her. 'And the people you're meeting?'

'Oh, them. They'd left a note at reception. Can't make it.'

Which lead to Marianne feeling that everything about Ricki had an air of mystery about it.

'Lucky for me, maybe?' he quickly added.

'Your accent. It's quite unique.'

'I'm not even sure myself what it is anymore,' he replied, 'I'm in Dunstable a hell of a long time now, so I guess it's by now a bit of a mixed bag, a bit like me, maybe.'

He smiled and she smiled back.

She was acutely aware how much she liked what she was feeling in this rather strange type of encounter. It was more like something she only ever saw perhaps in the movies instead of real life. It was different, but that in itself intrigued her.

'And yours?' he asked.

'My what?' she replied in a slightly flirtatious tone.

'Your name, what did you think I meant?' He laughed.

'Marianne,' she said, blushing, wishing she hadn't said that.

'That's a pretty name.'

'Sounds boring compared to Ricki.'

Ricki told her he lived over a bar he managed between Dunstable and London called The Traveller's Rest. He further shared in a low, important-sounding tone that he also ran a kind of off-the-record business as an agent for hostelries or individuals looking for bar staff, taxi drivers, bouncers and the like at short notice.

'Business is all about contacts and availability,' he said proudly.

'And which of those businesses brings you around here on the occasional Saturday morning?' she asked.

'My own,' he replied with a big grin, which she was not too happy about.

So when Ricki asked for her phone number, she declined, and when they had finished breakfast and he offered to drive her home, she equally declined.

'I like walking,' she said.

'I can see that.'

As she walked home, Marianne felt the whole encounter a bit like the first one, a bit weird and a lot surreal. So why was she feeling what she was feeling? Was it the whole opposites attract phenomenon, as in his apparent freedom compared to Charlie's entanglement with his daughter and Archie's commitment to his safe and single life, or was it the bold girl inside the disillusioned mature woman willing to be adventurous for a change? Was Ricki her Major Doryan – attractive, distant, brooding, exciting?

She realised that she had made a mountain of assumptions about him with no tangible evidence to support any of them. Feeling suddenly foolish, she realised that being a not bad looking recent widower, with this flashy car and his own business, he would have lots of admirers. He seemed interested in her in a way that would never reassure her. Was that his game? *Why, he never asked much about me or if I had a boyfriend,* she thought. She laughed at herself and the whole preposterous idea as she remembered her father telling her as a child that she had "notions above her station."

…chance of a lifetime…

To Charlie's disbelief, his callback by the college was not for a second interview, at least not the type he had been expecting. The college secretary welcomed him and gave him the good news that the college had decided to offer him a place on their Foundation Programme, but she added that this was not the only reason Liam and his business partner wanted to see him again, as she ushered him in to an artistically decorated but small room.

He was quickly joined by both parties, as they spoke about his honest interviews, both the one-to-one and within the group, his unique circumstances, his energy and willingness to remain motivated in times of hardship, his likeability and proven ability at sales, his creativity and his overall personality. In short, their main message to Charlie was, with his permission, the college would monitor his progress throughout his foundation programme, viewing it as some kind of a progression interview for a particular position within the college they were planning to fill. All of this was part of their advanced expansion plans outside of the capital. With a request that this conversation remained confidential, they wished him well in his immediate studies with the college.

Charlie began his foundation studies in Sept '87, loved every minute of it and was sad when it concluded in the following May. The course had opened his eyes and ears in so many ways that he would have loved the enlightenment process of continuing and growing in the Degree programme, particularly as his lecturers had warmly recommended him to the college as an ideal candidate for the same, but for Charlie the timing was bad. Mary Elizabeth's wellbeing and education had to come first and it all cost money and time, which is precisely what the Degree Programme would require in a way the Foundation Course had not. For Charlie, the decision was an easy decision, and so with a heavy heart he approached the college founder to enquire about a deferral of his continuing progression for now. Liam wanted to know why and was again reminded of Charlie's current family and financial situation, as outlined in his one-to-one interview.

Liam's response seemed unexpected, but as Charlie truly got to know the man over the coming years, it was less so.

'Have you forgotten what I said about this college perhaps having another option for you at some stage?'

Charlie had not forgotten but had assumed that completing the Degree Programme was an essential part of their thinking in this.

Liam continued. 'Ideally, yes. If you had the Degree completed, that would indeed have made things more straightforward, but we do not necessarily see it as a deal-breaker for now. As we briefly outlined previously, we are thinking of recruiting a good person with a recognised likeability factor to promote our profile outside of Dublin. Based on what we've observed during your foundation studies, we've decided to offer you as follows. If the college pays for you to complete an introductory part-time evening course in marketing while continuing in your own job, would you be interested in taking up our offer when it's completed? Once you begin working with us, the generous renumeration package includes a company car and full overnight accommodation allowance.'

Charlie didn't know what to say, so Liam just said, 'Think about it. We've come to know you here and we like you. We passionately believe that oftentimes we learn more from hardship than we do from success, and our college ethos is founded on that very principle. We see all of that in you. You know enough about our programmes from your foundation training and have a keen sense and strong values matching our ethos, which is especially important, and we think you are the man.'

Charlie was still speechless, so Liam continued.

'The training course we propose takes up about the same amount of time as the course you've successfully completed. We hope that, when this marketing training is complete, you will take up our job offer. You're still a young man and when in time your daughter makes her own way in the world, then you might consider returning to your degree studies, if that's still what you want.'

Charlie thought that there never had been a better offer made to him in his entire life, and it did not take him long to make his mind up. As he warmly shook Liam's hand, Charlie assured him that he would never let him or the college down.

'I know you won't,' was Liam's simple but gracious reply.

With Vera having become increasingly independent, he did not foresee any issues which wouldn't be compensated by the company car, meaning that Vera could have their old one all to herself, and the increased salary.

The only set-back in all of this was sharing his good news with Larry Broderick, but Larry quickly assured him there had been few conditions to his support.

'Every job has a shelf life, Charlie. You were the right man in the right place for us at the time and now you're the right man in the right place for this new and upcoming college.'

So the duration of Charlie's introduction to marketing studies acted as his notice to Larry, and as he hoped, the new promotion job turned out to be perfect for him. Sadly, sometime later due to ill-health, when Liam had to take a step back from the college, he ensured that Charlie's position was safe within the new ownership structure but asked him to promise he would one day complete his therapy training, which promise was freely given.

When, many years later, Liam sadly passed away, Charlie was asked if he would like to contribute to his memory.

He wrote the following with pride and gratitude.

The Man I knew as Liam

First day in college – didn't feel so good
At the top of the room, this gentleman stood
Where I felt I couldn't – he said I could
The man I knew as Liam
Compassion and kindness he brought to life
That everyone has the potential to thrive
Where shame and judgement no longer abide
The man I knew as Liam

Where others saw little, he saw a lot
"You're going to make it" is what he taught
Brought hope in a way it couldn't be bought
The man I knew as Liam
He showed that lives can be turned around
Where nurture and positive regard are found
Broken wings in time will leave the ground
The man I knew as Liam

He believed trials and hardships are only a test
There's no perfection without a mess
What a beautiful lesson, the very best
From the man I knew as Liam
A coach, a teacher, a mentor, a friend
Each time we met – something new to be learned
Where straight wouldn't fit, I was shown how to bend
By the man I knew as Liam

He refused to accept a simple "No"
There was always another way to go

And miracles happened for me, I know
From the man I knew as Liam
And in this tribute I am not removed
From the countless others whose lives he's moved
The core conditions surely proved
By the man I knew as Liam

He may never know just what he's done
To so many lives, but I'll speak for one…
…the author of this humble poem
To the man I knew as Liam

...bright side of the road...

In the meantime, Marianne's friendship with the choir gentleman continued to become more important to her with each passing week. Archie was a polite, well-read, interesting and knowledgeable man who worked as a librarian, which may have contributed to his having a fine mind. He drove an Austin Metro, what he described as a boring but safe car, and he liked driving. The fact that he was older than her, and she was taller than him, seemed to matter not to either of them. He was mostly available at weekends, so those days of loneliness had become occupational, educational and interesting days instead, very much to be looked forward to.

On chosen Saturdays they would visit places of interest, such as public parks, theatres, libraries, art galleries and museums, while on chosen Sundays they sang together in the choir before going for lunch and a stroll.

Archie shared that he had never married and enjoyed being his own man. He listened very intently to her story and felt that her life seemed quite tragic.

'Where do you believe your father is now?' he suddenly queried on one such Sunday stroll.

'I'd like to think that what the nuns taught us about heaven is true, but it's probably a bit far-fetched,' she answered.

'Why?'

'I'm not sure, to be honest.'

'Sometimes our ego gets in the way,' Archie replied.

Marianne was intrigued at this stage.

'Please tell me more,' she said.

'Just because our limited human minds cannot visualise a life without our human bodies, beyond our current understanding, doesn't necessarily mean it's not there.'

He had her attention, so he continued.

'Just a human example. When we dream, we can travel the world, while our bodies lie still in our beds.'

As they contemplated all of that, Marianne was fascinated by such thinking and by Archie's mind in general.

When she told him how she wished she had studied harder back home to get into college, he talked positively about the marvellous educational and career opportunities available now for mature students.

When she sounded really interested, he said he would conduct the relevant research for her, adding that he found it hard to believe she was alone, as unlike him, she hadn't chosen that path.

Marianne, intrigued with his comment, equally wondered to herself how a man with all his qualities and talents ended up alone, and being seemingly happy with that.

If I could arrive at that place, wouldn't it be wonderful, she thought. But she wasn't there yet.

With Archie, she in ways had the ideal situation, as in weekend company with an interesting man without the pressures, responsibilities and stresses of a relationship.

When she asked him about his relationship life, he went noticeably quiet for a while.

Then he said, 'There was someone once,' before adding that it was a long time ago and was long forgotten.

'I have a feeling there's much more to that story than you're saying.'

He reflectively replied, 'Perhaps there is, but it's from a forgotten era.'

'If ever you find the missing pieces, I'm a good listener,' she said softly.

'I know you are,' he said, leaving her feeling pretty good.

...hello darkness my old friend...

If there was anything worse than the Saturday morning grocery shopping, it was trying to do so by bus on a miserably cold and wet Saturday morning. This was one such Saturday morning, but eventually Marianne found herself in the bus shelter outside the shopping centre with her three full shopping bags, hoping the bus wouldn't be late.

She noticed the other people within the shelter suddenly take notice as one said, 'He can't park there,' as a car pulled into the bus stop and she heard that unmistakable accent again.

'Hello there.'

It was Ricki. Because he had directed his greeting specifically at her, the lady who had mentioned about the car parking in the bus bay decided to repeat the same statement to Marianne. Embarrassed, she walked out of the bus shelter and was heading off in the rain before he followed her, the car window at her side rolled down.

'Hello,' he said.

'You've embarrassed me,' she said in an annoyed tone of voice.

'I didn't mean to. I just wanted you to get in.'

With that, they both saw the bus pulling away, as he repeated, 'I still do.'

She felt she might as well, at least till the next bus came, feeling embarrassed at not looking exactly her best in the rain.

'So, what brings you this way this morning?' she sarcastically asked as she sat in and placed the bags at her feet.

'I met a policeman earlier and he didn't ask me that. But, seeing as how I've embarrassed you and caused you to miss your bus, the least I can do is to bring you home out of the rain.'

'There'll be another bus soon.'

'Are you always this stubborn?'

'Are you always going to turn up in my life, just like this, when I least want you to?'

'I hope so.' He smiled as they headed for the exit of the car park.

She still felt quite distracted as he chatted away, mostly boastful things about himself and his achievements, while not asking much her about her. Ten minutes later he pulled up outside 125 West St, when it suddenly dawned on her that he hadn't asked for her address. In an instant she felt uneasy, which quickly moved through the gears to fear, then to a most uncomfortable flight feeling in her body.

She quickly got out of the car, collected her groceries and thanked him.

Unperturbed by Marianne's sudden change in body-language, he gave his usual, 'See you around,' and drove off.

At this stage. Marianne wasn't at all sure if seeing Ricki around ever again was what she wanted anymore.

… this story has no home so I will tell it here…

"Two individuals sit in a room, talking. Welcome to a typical talk-therapy session. They are not alone. Pathways trampled by others from previous and current life events move through the room. The air buzzes with unseen voices and memories. Some are subtle entrances – invited – but others are uninvited guests and events that make noise as they enter – but will not be kept out. And the presence of all affects this meeting." (from M. Carroll. *Counselling Supervision*).

It had been a little over two years since his return from Dunstable and a little over three months since the replacement of his counselling training by training in marketing, and Charlie was well into honouring a suggestion from one of his counselling lecturers that perhaps it was time for his own therapy. The main aim of his therapy was derived from the title of John Powell's book, *Will the real me please stand up*. He chose a psychoanalyst, Frank, a man taller than he, with all the reflective characteristics of either a very boundaried individual, a professional psychoanalyst or an introvert, or possibly all three.

Charlie found himself checking the time as he pulled up outside a two-storey brick house in mid-August 1988, a week after his thirty-sixth birthday. Frank practiced from his home which was in the midst of a housing estate on the outskirts of a town twenty miles from Charlie's home village and reminded him in some ways of 125 West St.

There was nothing particularly special about the front of this house to make it stand out, no obvious sign as to what went on inside, no particular sense of felt healing as one looked at it from the outside. In one sense, it was like the other houses on the estate, except the other houses had nice gardens to their front, while this house had a sterile lawn without any further need for floral or horticultural decoration. In this, it matched Frank's style and that of his office, as if this sparse synchronicity was by design. He anxiously watched the seconds on his watch tick by as he had done on each of his ten sessions to date. His therapist had made it noticeably clear in their initial phone call that he didn't do either early or late.

Thus far into his therapy with Frank, it seemed Charlie had chosen well. And any further misgivings he had about this chosen form of therapy were firmly put to bed when, at the end of their second session, Frank abruptly stopped the flow of conversation to say, 'Can I tell you what I sense is happening here? You signed up to talk to me about your current internal conflicted state of mind, but what's developed has been more of an analytical discussion about this guy called Charlie between the two us, both of us perched safely in an observation station.'

When Charlie sought clarification, Frank explained.

'There should only be two people in this room, Client Charlie and Psychoanalyst Frank. But client Charlie hasn't spoken at all, hasn't been given a chance. What you're doing here is speaking from the present *about* Charlie in the past, not from a sacred hurt space *within* Charlie presently. This needs to change for your therapy to continue, meaning one of us has to come down from the observation post, and it won't be me.'

After that, it was different. Charlie's *real inside-out* therapy had begun.

He was now almost three months into very real and often painfully reflective therapy. He had pretty much gone through his entire life, including his childhood, his time at a tender age in a monastery, his marriage to Vera, and their child.

He was now pretty up to date with his life narrative, culminating in the entire Marianne saga, where he shared that it had all seemed almost pre-ordained. An unhappily married man with an eight-year-old daughter meets someone he once knew, an unlucky-in-love woman without child, of similar age to him, which he had interpreted as a scenario painted by angels, and therefore one to which he was perfectly entitled.

This was session number eleven and Charlie had concluded since his last session that he had enough of the past processed and wanted to use today's session to talk about the present and the future. He particularly wanted to explore his surprisingly conflicted feelings about Vera's increasing independence from him, and to an upsetting update he had heard regarding Marianne.

In his therapy sessions to date, Charlie had learned that he would be doing the majority of the talking. Frank sat behind the therapy couch and occasionally would be heard writing, but rarely involved himself in any actual dual dialogue, other than to give it the odd "steer" or seek context. Charlie understood that is what psychoanalysts do.

His thoughts were interrupted by his watch alarm indicating that it was time. He politely knocked, as was his way.

His knock was answered with an equally quiet, 'Come in, Charlie,' as was Frank's way.

Charlie entered, placed the session fee on Frank's locker and took his position on the couch, like the previous ten sessions.

Frank began by sharing that Charlie had mentioned at the end of their last session about an upsetting development from Dunstable, which he was hoping to check out. Charlie nodded and took a deep breath as he quoted Vera's bombshell to him ten days previously. 'That slapper in Dunstable has moved on.'

He went on to say that his body language must have given him away, for her next comment had been, 'I knew you hadn't gotten over her. And that's why you're living with your parents and that's where you'll be staying.'

When he had queried, 'How do you know?' he received an even more hurtful reply.

'That's for me to know and you to find out. He's younger than you and single. So, let that be a sharp lesson for you, and get her out of your head for good.'

During the next fifty minutes, Frank expertly processed all of that information, and its effect on his client, before he said the familiar, 'Is it ok if we leave it there?'

Charlie got off the therapy couch and they agreed to take a month's break, which would afford Charlie the space to carry out one or two pieces of planned research which he didn't share with Frank. It would be time enough to review the same in their next session, which would be a milestone session number twelve.

…if anything happened to you…

When Marianne met Archie after choir on the Sunday after the latest encounter with Ricki, she was tempted to share the entire Ricki story with him. Perhaps he could put a less threatening perspective on Ricki's knowledge of where she lived. But she decided against telling him and as their conversation developed over lunch, she was glad of her decision.

She noticed that he was quieter than usual, so when she asked if there was something on his mind, his face assumed a sad smile.

When she smiled back with a quizzical look, he thought long and hard before answering.

'I don't like feeling vulnerable,' he said.

'Vulnerable is not a word I'd usually associate with you, Archie.'

'I'm feeling vulnerable right now.'

'Why?' she asked too quickly, wishing she had allowed him to say more. 'Seems to me you have your life down to a fine art, an independent man who likes living alone, a man with more meaning and interests in life than any other man I know.'

Archie thought for a long time.

Then he said, 'You have become a very significant presence in my life.'

'As you have in mine.'

'Maybe that's where my vulnerability lies.'

'I don't understand.'

'I've grown to really like you, Marianne, and our times together have become an incredible addition to my life.'

'As yours has to mine.'

'But I have allowed something to happen that I had vowed would never happen again. I have developed strong feelings for you.'

'As I have for you,' she replied, again too quickly.

'So, I began thinking of how it would be if that guy Charlie were to return, or you were to meet another younger man.'

'That hasn't bothered you up until this point.'

'Please, hear me out. In all probability, you may well have needs that, with the best of intentions, I cannot meet.'

'Like what?'

'Like youth, energy, nightlife, excitement.'

'Why now?'

'Now I feel I have something to lose.'

Was Archie a mind-reader, she thought to herself.

He continued, choosing his words carefully. 'I don't want to lose you. Yet it doesn't feel it's right to tie you down.'

'Perhaps I can be the best judge of that.'

'I guess, in an old-fashioned way, I'm asking you how you would feel about you and I becoming committed companions.'

'Do you mean a relationship?'

'I guess so,' he answered, sounding very unsure.

Marianne hesitated.

'Promise me you'll think about it,' he said.

Marianne nodded. 'Of course I will.'

'Good,' he said with a sense of relief to have the conversation over for now.

'Now, where would you like to eat today?'

When Archie dropped her home later that evening, she thought that his proposition to her wasn't exactly in the running for romantic gesture of the year. In a moment of black humour, she reckoned that if they were to get married, Archie the librarian would probably organise the invited guests on the day to be seated under "categories of interest" or in alphabetical order.

In doing this, she realised she was probably rationalising the fact that she was probably leaning towards something a

148

bit more exciting. The minute that thought entered her head, she realised what an astute man Archie really was, and it didn't feel good.

…if the mountain doesn't come to Mohammed…

Marianne instinctively knew this was probably not her best idea, and she equally knew it could constitute what her father would call *playing with fire*, but she would reason it by calling it research. She remembered how, amongst Ricki's many boasts, was that of his privileged position as manager of The Traveller's Rest. She would call there unexpectedly, probably find out they had never heard of Mr Ricki, and that would be the end of that. And perhaps then, she might be free to view Archie's proposal in a better light.

Ricki was unfinished business, but not for long more, she thought. On the following Saturday night, she paid a bit more than usual attention to her appearance before ordering a taxi.

As she got out of the taxi she noticed the bright lights, loud music and overall liveliness of the place, far removed from the places she and Archie frequented. Was this what he had meant in referencing her "younger woman needs" she wondered.

On entering what to her looked like a tavern, her eyes slowly adjusted to the darkened atmosphere inside. The place was pretty full. As can be the case with any woman who enters a place like this on her own, Marianne was feeling the heat of every pair of eyes as she tried to navigate her way to the one vacant seat she could see, where she was immediately approached by one of the on-floor waitresses.

'Will you be needing a second seat?' she was asked before indicating she was ok with the one.

'What can I get you?'

'A gin and tonic please,' she said, not sure if in fact she should be drinking, for it had been a long time since she had experienced the warm but calming feeling that alcohol can bring.

But by now, that efficient waitress was halfway across the floor to fulfil her order. She thought about making a brief enquiry about Ricki when her drink was delivered but thought better of it. Better to observe, she thought.

If she didn't see him within ten minutes, she would take it as a sign. There was a certain relief in that escape plan, but of course, precisely ten minutes later she saw him enter, only to find there was an attractive woman by his side, younger than him, laughing together as they entered.

Leave now before he sees you, was her first reaction. But it was too late, for the minute Ricki went behind the bar, he saw her and immediately came down to her.

'What's this?' he asked.

'What does it look like?' she answered.

'So, it's true what they say about people who answer a question with a question.' He laughed. 'Are you alone?'

'Are you?' she replied.

'There we go again.'

'Well, are you?'

'I asked you first.' He laughed again.

'I saw you come in,' she added very pointedly.

'Oh, you mean the woman that came in with me?'

'Do I?'

Marianne wanted to sound as if she did not care, which was anything but the truth.

'One of the staff here.' He brushed her query away lightly. 'Her car wouldn't start on the busiest night of the week, of all nights.'

'And you just had to be the good Samaritan?'

The words were out of her mouth before she realised her tone sounded just like that of a jealous wife.

'It's business,' he corrected her.

There seemed to be a game of cat and mouse developing, so Marianne decided to change the subject.

'It's quite the place you manage here.'

'It can be,' he replied. 'Hey, it's so lovely to see you, but I'm down a second staff member, so I'm afraid I'm on duty. Would you like another drink on me?'

'No thanks,' she said, trying to maintain the upper lip.

'Can I see you again?' he asked, surprising her.

'If you like' she said, with an apparent nonchalance she certainly wasn't feeling.

'Next Friday night,' he replied. 'You have my business card. Call me during the week, yeah?'

He was obviously in a hurry, so she was not going to make a nuisance of herself. After all, it had been her choice to arrive unexpectedly.

'Go,' she said and he quickly returned behind the bar without a second invitation.

She finished her drink and left as quietly as she came in.

In the taxi back home, she tried to process both her motivation and her madness. Her anxious entrance, wondering why he wasn't there, her surprise when he did arrive, relief at his apparently being pleased to see her, disappointment that he was busy, happy that he wanted her to call him regarding meeting up on Fri night. But would she? Should she? What about Archie?

When she woke the following morning, she noticed that her apprehension was far greater than her excitement. But she was happy that, for once, she had entered Ricki's world by surprise instead of the other way round. And she had his number and he didn't have hers. She comforted herself that she would not call him. She had got all she wanted from the visit to The Traveller's Rest. Or had she?

Would she tell Archie when they were due to meet later? She thought not, but did he have a right to know? He seemed to not carry any secrets, so why did she need to? She decided to do nothing for now. After all she was not going to call Ricki, so there was nothing to tell.

But human needs move more like a skilled dancer than a static monument. The need for safety and companionship

152

today can morph into the need for excitement, intimacy and risk tomorrow.

Once more, Marianne became acutely aware of the theme of *Ryan's Daughter* running through her own life. Archie was warm, kind, interested, and brought out the best in her, just like the teacher Mr Shaughnessy in the film, while Ricki was and did pretty much the exact opposite, just like Major Doryan. The problem for Rosie Ryan was that the Major could touch her and move her internally in a way the teacher could not.

Marianne's conflict was pretty much the same. She knew what she felt for Ricki was dangerous, a feeling from her shadow side, something more akin to addiction. But whatever it was, her craving for "let's see where it goes" pulled her so strongly by Wednesday of that week that she called the number on Ricki's card.

When he suggested a well-known upmarket restaurant, she insisted on a bar and restaurant that she was more familiar with, where she knew some of her workmates might be on a Friday evening. She would be assertive and keep the risk to a minimum.

He did not seem too happy at her choice before saying he had to go. He would collect her Friday evening at seven o'clock.

Her humorous, 'Sure, you know where I live,' brought a sarcastic laugh, which she didn't like.

And besides, she felt disappointed that he had to go. She had been looking forward to a decent conversation wherein she could have broached the subject of how he knew where she lived, but it seemed it wouldn't ever be like that with Ricki.

…into the lion's den…

It was the Friday after Marianne's visit to The Traveller's Rest and, as she began her familiar trek home from work, she noticed her tolerance with the whole bus mode of transport had dwindled. As a result, she'd decided to take driving lessons.

But was it her lack of tolerance of the stop-start bus or her anxiety about her date with Ricki that had her so edgy?

And of course, when she got home, she was suddenly thrown into the old familiar panic. *What should I wear?*

Although Ricki seemed dead keen on her when they first met, his hot and cold ways were now beginning to make her question herself about what he felt towards her. She decided it was time to find out.

She arrived home, showered and began trawling through her wardrobe, looking for something that might turn his head.

She pulled out a pair of slacks and a strappy top. No, too casual. Next a wrap dress. No, too tight. A jumpsuit? No, too frumpy. A skirt? No, too old fashioned. Panic was now setting in with the old familiar "Everything looks terrible on me" routine, when from the corner of her eye she spotted her red dress and thought to herself *this will impress him*.

The next conflict area was the shoes: strappy sandals, stilettos or chunky shoes? Wait, how tall was he again? More panic. And, right in the middle of the panic, of course she had a flashback of Charlie's observant comment on the number of shoes she actually kept on his first visit to 125 West St.

She decided to have a glass of wine to get Charlie out of her head and out of the moment, before eventually settling on the strappy sandals, applying her make-up and lastly, but by no means leastly, generously applying her favourite perfume. Reaching into her jewellery box, as she picked out the pearl necklace that she had bought from her first pay cheque, she spotted the bracelet that Charlie had brought her on his initial one-day visit to Dunstable.

The memory of the shoes and the bracelet slightly threw her. She realised she was preparing to go out with another man, adding to her existing guilt about Archie, but then she thought, What the hell, Charlie's doing what he has chosen to do and Archie is probably at home watching *University Challenge* on TV. Its time I did something I want. She chose however to assuage her guilt by not wearing Charlie's bracelet.

Ricki arrived on time and the look in his eyes at the front door told her she had chosen well. She had to admit in that moment that she liked the feeling of being wanted as an attractive woman in that way, had missed it, needed it and it was a good start to her first real night out in a long time. Of course, Ricki knew the taxi driver and again, when they arrived at her chosen venue, he seemed equally at home there, chatting freely to the bartenders as he ordered their drinks. All barmen know all bars, she thought, and then she remembered his extra-curricular business and it all made sense.

They ordered food and, as she was enjoying her drink, he excused himself to talk to two of the bartenders and a fellow who looked like a bouncer, while she was left on her own. She watched him chatting away happily with his mates, or were they all staff of his, and using his considerable charm with the ladies while not even once looking in her direction.

But on his return he explained that yes, they were people who collaborated with him sometimes in his bar and sometimes in his other business, and she thought that sounded fair enough. He paid her full attention once their food arrived and during further drinks. After, he hailed a taxi again, one of his own people, which meant there was no waiting. This made her feel special.

Ricki took her to a hotel he seemed to know very well that night, perhaps too well, Marianne thought. If she should have shared her concern, she chose not to, as they mutually agreed not to delve into past lovers.

...the truth is rarely pure and never simple...

After his last therapy session, Charlie thought long and hard about what to do next. There was a strong need growing inside him to return to Dunstable for a few days, just to look around if nothing else. His new job would enable such a visit without jeopardy, so his mind was made up.

Hoping that Marianne was still at the same address, Charlie took to the pen again, outlining his current circumstances, both personal and work-wise, and hoping she was well. Like the letter he had written to her what seemed a lifetime ago, he added that if she was happily getting on with her life, making no reference to Vera's statement, she could shred this letter and she would never hear from him again. But on the off-chance that was not the case, if for closure's sake if nothing else, he would so like for them to meet up, even if he knew he had little right to make such a request.

Meanwhile, back in Dunstable, that Friday night set the trend for Marianne's dates with Ricki which were, like himself, forever undependable. The warm and pleasurable connection that night in the hotel was followed by radio silence for several days. This was to become the pattern.

It seemed that, in Ricki's world, a relationship meant something more resembling fifty first dates than her idea of one. Granted, she enjoyed how much he wanted her, not to mention the grand gestures, like when she told him about the driving lessons, he had a small but perfect car delivered to her door on the very next Saturday morning with a big bow on the driver's door.

But while displaying excitement and gratitude, deep inside she would have preferred if he had sat down with her to talk seriously about their future. But Ricki was Ricki, and she very much doubted that she occupied his mind as much as he did hers, or that he wouldn't prefer to stick needles in his eyes than have that conversation with her.

She had decided that at this point Archie deserved to know the truth. On their next walk, she shared the full Ricki story with him, while assuring him that their friendship was sacred. Archie went noticeably quiet as they strolled the beautiful grounds of a church he had taken her to on that Sunday afternoon.

'And what if I can't do it?' he said.

'Sorry?' she said.

'Friendship under those circumstances, I mean.'

'I don't understand,' she said.

'When I shared about my feelings with you and hoped we could come up with some type of committed relationship, I felt you seemed open to the idea. So this is a bit of a bombshell, to be honest.'

'I know' she said quietly, 'but I hope we can remain friends, just like we've been.

'I don't think so,' he said slowly. 'I realise now you may not be as available as you had been, that you have commitments elsewhere. It will not be the same and I am not sure how that sits with me. I have a lot to think about.'

Marianne deliberately looked away as Archie continued.

'That day, when I spoke with you around the strong possibility of something like this actually happening, I was beginning to feel needy and vulnerable in a way I had not expected and was trying to see where I stood. Now I know, and I possibly feel a bit misled. So I will be retiring from the choir after next Sunday's Mass.'

Of all the low feelings Marianne had ever experienced, she reached a new level on hearing this.

'Please don't leave the choir,' she said. 'I'll leave.'

Through her tears she told him she didn't know where this situation with Ricki was going, if anywhere, and pleaded with him to change his mind about continuing their meetings.

'No, I had planned for this possibility. I'll leave you alone to pursue this relationship with Ricki. It may burn itself out and, if it does, I would love to hear from you again, but not till then.'

With that he walked away.

As she stood there, forlorn in the graveyard grounds, Marianne realised she was truly on her own again. She instantly decided she would leave the choir that day. Archie deserved at least that much, she thought as she made her way to their church.

After she had resigned from the choir, face to face, to one of the members who happened to be cleaning the church on that particular day, it hit her that she had lost Archie and the choir. And it was all because of Ricki.

But after an hour's crying, she suddenly felt anger towards Archie. Their friendship had a "no conditions" base, so what was his problem? And whatever his issue was, maybe that was the issue that led to him being on his own all along.

This anger comforted her for a while, but inevitably that strong feeling of loss resurrected and the need to find out more about Ricki's plans suddenly became even more urgent. Without thinking it through, she firmly told Ricki she wanted to meet him on the following Friday evening at the same bar as she had chosen for their first date.

Once more she went to great rounds to look well and feel confident. But, instead of receiving the answers she desperately needed, the big question marks about Ricki began to cement themselves ever deeper in earnest on that night.

And sure enough, same as their first date there, Ricki had collected her on time and been all attentive at first, but then had gone to join the bartenders and bouncers as previously, ignoring her and making no effort to introduce her.

After a time, seeing her alone, one of the guys from her workplace came over to her. Unfortunately, the timing was not exactly ideal for it was his birthday, and he was very obviously celebrating a bit too much. He was leaning in really close to Marianne as they spoke, and she saw Ricki's attention suddenly switching on.

And when her work colleague stumbled and grabbed her, bringing them both to the ground, she saw Ricki's face turn to thunder as he returned and insisted that his two colleagues bring her drunken friend home, which Marianne accepted at face value to be a kind gesture. At the end of the night, Ricki got a taxi to drop her home, saying there was something urgent he had to take care of.

But she was alarmed by the news at work on the following Monday that her work colleague had ended up in hospital, with no memory of how he got there. At first Ricki seemed annoyed when she asked him about it, but said he would check it out and get back to her. When he did, he assured her his friends had dropped her colleague home safely as he had said. It was his opinion that, in his drunken state, the guy must have gone back out again and said things he should not have said to the wrong kind of people.

After that incident, her work colleague group tried to steer her away from Ricki. But she did the exact opposite and steered away from them. It was not fair to blame him, she thought, for the stupid antics of their drunken colleague.

But Ricki's behaviour became even more erratic. On occasions, he cancelled plans at short notice, citing trouble at the bar as the usual reason. She had to ask herself if this was really what she wanted.

She concluded that she needed to make plans for her life going forward and requested that they meet for a serious conversation.

He agreed on a time and a date, but just as she was expecting him, he phoned to say he'd had a few drinks and would not be in a position to drive. When she told him that she would drive to meet at wherever he was, he said that could be awkward, leading her to conclude that he was probably with another woman. He proposed that they meet on the following evening in her home.

As only a woman desperate for affirmation can feel, she thought at last he seemed as serious about them as she was. Marianne based this untruth to herself on the basis that he wanted to meet her in her home, which was a pleasant change from his fondness of meeting in bars, where serious conversations are easily avoided.

So much so, that when an unexpected letter from Charlie arrived on that Friday morning, something she would have given her right arm for two years earlier, her feeling was one of such annoyance that she barely opened and glanced at it before throwing it on the worktop without even putting it back in the envelope, saying aloud to herself, 'Sorry Charlie, I don't believe anything has really changed and it probably never will. You made your bed almost three years ago.'

And with that, she dismissed Charlie from her mind, which truly reflected the power Ricki had over her.

That night she again dressed in clothes Ricki liked her to wear. He had told her repeatedly he loved her to dress in very feminine clothes that would show off her figure and her long legs. And on the few occasions she was too tired to dress in that way, he showed his displeasure and left early.

So tonight she was pleased that she had made the effort, and she became even happier that not only did he arrive, but he was early. She eagerly anticipated the look of approval which he would normally give and wondered if their conversation might have to wait till he would show her how much he appreciated how she looked, which occasionally happened, and which she was ashamed to admit she sometimes enjoyed.

But she also knew this meeting would probably be a deal breaker one way or the other. It could be the beginning of something or the end of something. So, on her way home from work, she had bought the perfect accompaniment to either a celebration or a heartache, a good bottle of wine.

Back in Ireland, Charlie waited for a reply to his letter, not knowing whether Marianne had moved house, moved on or both. Before their agreed break, his therapist had always urged him to see all actions as choices, each with its potential possibilities, good and bad. And even if the intended purpose of that action did not materialise, or hadn't turned out as well as was intended, it didn't mean the choice or action was an incorrect one and he must remain happy with his decision to do it.

This gave him time to review his own situation once again as it was. His parents seemed happy to have him living under the roof of his childhood, and his company car gave Digger some badly needed respite. His father still chose Digger's company, but his mother availed of Charlie's driving skills when needed, which was kept to a minimum, mostly to Mass and Devotions and to the Mission Days in a renowned religious centre nearby.

If Maggie was sad about his situation, she never said. Neither did she ever ask questions about his future and had seemingly tutored Martin likewise. Mary Elizabeth was a regular visitor, but Vera sadly did not darken their door.

He asked himself why he had written to Marianne at this stage. Would he be ok if she didn't reply or replied in anger? Or what if, as he had suggested in his letter, she wanted to meet him?

Had he allowed for all the possibilities of his reach-out letter? Was he willing to upset his child, his parents, again? Slowly but surely the village were forgetting the events of two and a half years ago and were accepting him back. Could he risk losing all of that again? And if he couldn't, what was he doing writing to Marianne?

He eventually concluded that he simply had to know the truth or otherwise of Vera's statement.

...because we couldn't see the
writing on the wall ...

With a reasonable degree of accuracy, one could have predicted that Marianne's "where are we going" conversation with Ricki would not go well. But to a woman whose head's been turned, it was still a surprise, when as was often the case with Ricki, it became quickly obvious to her that he had been drinking. He chose to remain standing as she found him both evasive and abrasive when she referred to their awkward phone call on the night he'd let her down. But her raising that subject seemed to trigger something dark and deep within him as their meeting took an ugly turn.

'We should just call it quits,' he said, before adding, 'this is getting too serious for me. You're a bit too serious for me. Besides, what is the fucking rush about knowing where we're going?'

Being in the presence of this dark side of Ricki, which she often felt was there but had previously not seen close up, scared Marianne.

But somehow she managed to remain calm.

'Every woman likes to know where she stands.'

'Don't give me that *every woman* shit!' he shouted.

She didn't reply.

'Is there someone else on the scene, is that it?'

Marianne was not having any of it.

'Should that not be my line?'

'I don't think that's any of your fucking business, do you?'

'It is if you and I are to have a future,' she said, knowing she was walking here on rather thin ice, but if this meeting was to be a defining one, there seemed little point in playing safe.

Ricki's voice-tone returned to one of calm and deliberation, which Marianne felt was even more worrying.

'I just don't get what all the fucking urgency is about,' he said as he turned as if to leave, 'unless, as I said, you're looking elsewhere.'

Marianne's not immediately feeding his ego at this point didn't go down well.

'We're done,' he said angrily.

'Just like that?' she said.

'Just like that. I spend most of my days working hard and being answerable to people, but I always considered my nights to be my own. But not so, according to you, so we'll just leave it. I'll get one of the boys to collect the car over the next few days.'

As he moved towards the door, his eye caught the open letter on the worktop, and before she could move, he had Charlie's letter in his hand, reading it. Her attempt to take it from him was met with a closed fist pointing towards her face.

'I was fucking right!' he shouted triumphantly, glancing at Charlie's letter.

'You're not right!' she shouted back. 'He just randomly sent that letter without invitation from me.'

'Randomly, my bollox.' Ricki had by now lost the plot. 'You couldn't wait to have him back.'

'No,' she protested in vain as she wondered why she was even bothering at this stage, for Ricki was only beginning his final rant.

'I can't fucking believe that you're getting back with that nerdy geek with the little blonde girl you had here.'

Marianne suddenly found courage from somewhere.

'How did you know about them?'

'You must have told me.'

But Marianne was adamant.

'No, we agreed not to discuss previous relationships, remember?'

'Well, someone must have told me.'

'No one told you, because no one knew,' she said calmly.

At this exposure, Ricki stiffened with rage, saw the bottle of wine on the side table and threw it against the wall with such force that it broke into pieces.

'So, you want to get back with that weakling?' he shouted.

'I didn't say that, and he wasn't weak.'

'He wasn't weak.' Ricki sneeringly imitated her. 'Tell me this, then, what man would crumple, after one soft blow, and let his little daughter be snatched by people in balaclavas neither he nor she knew?'

Marianne was shocked, so when she spoke it was in a quiet angry voice that she hardly recognised as her own.

'So that's how you knew where I lived.'

Ricki was suddenly chillingly cool again and nodded.

'I watched you getting on that bus every morning for a week beforehand and saw Mr Weakling and the child leave later afterwards for school. We had to get our times exactly right.'

Marianne felt this was perhaps her only chance to know more.

'What was in it for you?'

'An old debt that had to be paid,' he said, vaguely but gravely.

'So the entire horror of that morning was all about you repaying a debt?'

Ricki nodded and she continued.

'The debt was paid off at that point. So why did you pursue me?'

'There was more.'

'More?'

'A bonus.'

Marianne was beginning to feel something she didn't like, as Ricki continued.

'I would receive a sizeable cash bonus if I could get you into bed and provide proof.'

A terrible frightening truth dawned on Marianne as if she'd been suddenly pushed under an ice-cold shower.

'So, you weren't really looking for a church at all that morning?'

Ricki began to laugh before becoming boastful again.

'I continued to follow your movements after lover boy's desertion, but waited a time to make my move. And before you even ask, I didn't have the faintest clue who the funeral Mass was for on that morning. That idea only came to me when I saw how vulnerable and available you were, like a ripe grape on the vine.'

Marianne was drowning in a sea of her own shame but she just had to know more.

'You mentioned having to provide proof of my successful seduction, shall we call it?'

Ricki's response was unemotional.

'There was a recorder in that hotel room.'

At this, Marianne vomited into the kitchen sink, but from somewhere found the courage to continue.

'So, with your bonus earned, why didn't you leave it at that?'

Ricki went quiet for a time and, when he spoke, his voice had softened.

'Besides winning the bonus, something happened in the hotel room that night.'

'Meaning?'

'I found I really liked you, felt something I hadn't previously felt with any woman, and wanted to again.'

'But on your terms only.'

That reply did not go down at all well. Ricki's voice changed again, as if he was angry with himself for revealing his vulnerability. He stood up to his full height, face red with anger.

'Look at the state of you. Seeing you now, I have to ask myself were you worth all the bother? And the answer is: Fuck, no!'

Marianne's voice sounded stronger than she felt.

'You got what you wanted, you got me to bed, you won your bonus. Store those memories away well, for that privilege will never be yours again. If I've been such a major disappointment to you, you have been my greatest mistake.'

Ricki's reaction startled her as he hit her hard across the face with his closed fist and grabbed her tightly by the throat.

'I'll never have you again, eh?' he sneered through clenched teeth. 'Well, we'll see about that, won't we.'

He wrestled her onto the rug on the floor, roughly holding her right hand in his left while pulling up her dress with his right hand.

Somehow, from the corner of her left eye, Marianne spotted a large piece of the broken wine bottle which thankfully seemed within reach, the piece with the most jagged end. She secured the safe end of the bottle in her hand and thrust the broken end in the direction of Ricki's right eye with all her might.

'You bitch!' he roared as he jumped up and grabbed a tea towel to try and stem the flow of blood.

She saw her chance to break free and fled upstairs and locked herself in the bathroom. She could hear him cursing as he followed her, breathing heavily as he banged against the door.

'Let me in, you bitch. You've fucking blinded me!'

As she became gripped in fear for what seemed like a lifetime, she heard him go back down the stairs and use her landline, instructing someone to come and collect him immediately. Marianne, praying like she had never prayed before, collapsed onto the bathroom floor in relief and gratitude when she heard the front door close.

She eventually got herself to bed but lay fearfully awake all night. She knew she would not be leaving the house again for a few days at least. She had no idea where to turn to, so she picked up Charlie's letter again, which concluded with, "in which case, Marianne, I will leave you in peace."

She could not but notice the irony of the last two words in his letter. If only he knew, she thought, I've never been as far away from peace as I am right in this moment. But she equally knew that she could not afford to take any shelter in this letter of Charlie's, as she remembered her vow to never put anyone through the pain that had been inflicted on so many people back then. If she did reply, it would be out of courtesy. That window had been well and truly closed.

She then called her Aunt Julie to say she needed to come home for a while as soon as possible to sort things out. As ever, Julie was delighted to hear from her, assured her that she was always welcome to stay with her for as long as she needed, and that she could even step straight back into her job if she cared to. Marianne was afraid to say any more over the phone because she no longer trusted Ricki and his ability to interfere in her life and there was a strong sense that he didn't do unfinished business. She even stupidly thought of getting herself a wig and dark glasses for going outdoors but instantly remembered that disguises were something Ricki knew quite a lot about.

...the leather graveyard...

After three weeks of fading hope, Charlie was pleasantly surprised when Marianne's reply arrived. In it she stated that she had plans to return to her aunt in Ireland and that she would meet him at the same garden centre as previously on a particular date and time.

She gave him just one date and one time, Saturday the 6th of May, 1989, which was coming up to three years since he had arrived with his child in Dunstable. She added that they would be meeting as friends, stating *too much water has flown under that particular bridge*.

Charlie intuitively knew he would be there to meet her. The days of fatal hesitation were behind him.

The weather on that Saturday morning matched Charlie's mood, with a pleasant breeze blowing beneath a clear blue sky, as he headed to the garden centre where the seeds of their second chance at romance had blossomed. Remembering what she had said in her letter about water under the bridge, and that it was their first time for them to meet since his walking out on her, he knew their encounter today would be, if anything, of the healing variety, or so he hoped.

He found himself caught between being pleased she had agreed to meet him and jointly terrified about what she might want to say to him. Vera had assured him that Marianne had moved on. Was she right? How would she know? Would he be strong enough to hear that if it were true?

When he arrived, he was delighted to see Marianne already there waiting at that same bus stop. She was alone, which allayed his main concern. From his initial view she looked as beautiful as ever, but once he got nearer he thought he saw bruise marks on her throat. She must have noticed him noticing, for she instantly offered 'a little medical procedure' as an upfront explanation. If Charlie had been hoping this would have acted as an ice breaker, it didn't seem to do that and he could feel the tension between them rising as they walked.

So he tried to break the tension by admiring her shoes and wondered if they were from her collection of shoes he had drafted a poem about after his one-day visit to Dunstable.

'Very funny' she replied.

As they walked nonchalantly through the multi-coloured flower beds, Charlie was for once glad of the circumstances of talking to someone while not looking directly at them. The conversation was slow and expectedly laboured by the time they reached a beautifully ornate outdoor seating area along by the river, where Marianne indicated they might sit.

Charlie immediately remembered the last time they had sat by a river. If Marianne remembered, she did not say and Charlie did not particularly want to raise it. But when he saw the nearby shop he could not resist excusing himself, indicating he was going to the toilet before hopping over the low wall between the river and the shop and returning proudly with two choc ices.

'No sign of Bro James, thank God,' he assured her, still trying to lighten the atmosphere.

Marianne did not reply and slowly began to open the choc ice, but at some point between opening it and eating it, seemed to have had as much of the small talk as she could stomach.

'Have you any idea what it was like for me to find your letter back then after a horrible day at work?'

There was no reply from Charlie.

'But, then again, you had form at this type of desertion. After all, you left an identical letter for your poor wife to find only seven weeks previously. And, in case you think I am, I'm not entirely blind to the ironic karma in all of that.'

Charlie continued to remain silent.

170

'But the worst part for me,' she continued, 'was that the night before you left, I took you to my bed to comfort both of us. That comfort turned into something beautiful, but something beautiful that would mean I could have been carrying your baby on the day you left. But you didn't think about that, did you, or if you did, you didn't seem to care.'

She was now crying as Charlie continued to seek refuge in silence, till he too became upset.

'I'm so sorry, I really am. I've spent months in therapy, trying to understand who I was back then, or who I became.'

'And have you?'

Charlie felt there were no further escape hatches.

'No, I can't explain or excuse any or all of my actions during that time. So, to answer your reasonable question, I have not come to try and defend myself, but rather to seek your forgiveness and to see if we might at least try to come to some kind of terms around it.'

'So, what you are now telling me is that you only put a *pause* on us to make us both stronger, believing that at any stage you could press the *play* button again.'

Charlie was struggling.

'I know how much I wronged you, but I still believe with a passion that I can make it up to you. I genuinely believe that.'

Marianne wondered if he only knew what he was offering, but decided to say no more for now.

Charlie knew his timing was not the best, but the question had been forming in his mouth ever since the moment they'd met.

'Is it true you've met someone else?'

The mere question sent shivers simultaneously down both Marianne's and Charlie's spines.

'Who told you?'

'Vera,' he blurted out, but immediately recognising that wasn't the cleverest thing for him to do, attempted a retreat. 'But I don't understand how she could possibly know.'

'Oh, you'd be surprised at what she knows and how she knows it,' was Marianne's cryptic response, leaving Charlie more confused than ever.

Meeting Charlie's need to move the conversation on was clearly far from being top of Marianne's list in that moment.

'I have no intention of explaining anything or everything I had to do to survive your walking out on me, to you or to anyone else. In making your choice, you gave up all rights to know anything about mine.'

Charlie had the good sense to remain silent on the matter, even if Marianne did not.

'Were you disappointed to hear it?' she asked.

'It nearly killed me.'

But if was sympathy he was after, he was in the wrong place.

'So, you thought I would just accept my lot in life as a single woman and remain in some kind of emotional limbo for your complications to disappear and we'd all live happily ever after?'

Charlie felt it safer not to even attempt to answer that.

'I got on with my life, Charlie, because you left me no choice. Now that your life has freed up somewhat, although I am not totally convinced that to be the case if push came to shove again, it seems you are checking out to see where I'm at, to see if I can be put back on the list as one of your live options. Would you say that could be a reasonable summary of your letter?'

Charlie nodded. 'I can see why you might think that.'

Once again, Marianne seemed to soften, watching Charlie struggle so much.

'I want you to know that I did understand why you had to return to Ireland. The circumstance became quite bizarre, quite impossible, something beyond both our control.'

'That's very decent of you,' Charlie said.

Marianne reflected for a long time before speaking again.

'Sometimes,' she said, 'any of our circumstances can alter so much that we have to do something drastic to manage them.'

'Sounds like you're speaking from experience,' Charlie said softly.

'Not a conversation for now, Charlie. But what it all means is that I will be returning to Ireland permanently at some stage soon. And before you say anything about that news, I need to say this. Things seem to have improved for you since we last met. Sadly, the same cannot be said for me.'

Impulsive Charlie did not hesitate.

'Whatever it is, I want to be involved. I want to help. I owe you.'

If she was impressed with his enthusiasm, she didn't show it.

'I feel this is something I have to do alone, but I do promise that when I'm settled back here in Ireland, I will contact you.'

Charlie smiled as Marianne rose and they slowly made their way back to the bus stop.

As they passed Charlie's car, he briefly excused himself as he stopped and grabbed a wrapped present from it.

'For you,' he said softly.

Marianne remained silent for a while, before saying, 'Not till you give me some idea as to what's in it.'

Charlie understood her reticence.

'It's that poem, the one about the shoes. I really hope you can accept it.'

She gently took the package and gave him a hug. With that, her bus came and Charlie watched as she boarded and took her seat. She waved, which he took as his cue to leave.

He got into his car, not once looking back, but feeling pretty good. While he had not heard her say there was no one else, he got a sense that whoever or whatever it had been, it may have fizzled out.

...is it ever over and done...

When Marianne arrived back at her aunt's house from the garden centre, Julie immediately noticed the wrapped present and was curious.

'Treat yourself?' she asked.

Marianne decided it was time to be truthful about her day out, and why she had insisted on going alone, which led to two chairs been drawn up and the kettle being put on.

A full hour's conversation led to Marianne sharing about Charlie's present.

'When he first came over alone on a day trip, he was amazed at my shoe collection.'

Julie laughed. 'Most men would be, I imagine.'

'Anyhow, he'd written a poem about it at the time, but between one thing and another, the time was never right to give it to me. Till now.'

Julie's curiosity was now aroused.

'Are you not going to open it?'

'You open it,' Marianne said.

Julie didn't hesitate at the invitation and suddenly there were ribbons and wrapping being ripped off and, at last, the poem was revealed in its golden frame with non-glare glass. Julie was immediately impressed.

'Non-glare glass. The boy has gone to huge rounds and huge expense,' she said admiringly, as she handed it back to Marianne. 'Read it.'

'Will you read it?' Marianne asked.

'Are you sure?'

'Yes, I'm sure, please.'

Julie didn't need any further permission as she picked up the poem.

'He's called it The Leather Graveyard. How original and full of mystery,' she said, staring at it. Julie read it out.

The Leather Graveyard

Side by side they stand ... in military precision... each pair having once or twice haughtily flaunted their day in the sun ... the chosen ones ... glowing in the promise of eternal life ... which was but a brief flurry of glory ... till rendered redundant by the media-driven forces and frenzy of fashion ... preferred term; retail therapy ... now locked away in cold storage, they wait ... like unwanted dogs in a shelter ... waiting to be claimed ... to be filled once more by those beautiful, shapely legs they had once adorned ... how could they have been forgotten ... such a spectacular fall from grace ... what had they done ... had they hurt you ... had their heels let you down as you determinedly strode the catwalk of high rise apartments ... And so lifelessly they remain ... wishing they could be resurrected from this place ... by other feet who would appreciate them ... feet of those who don't need or can't afford the luxury of gratuitous choice ... grateful faithful feet ... but forgotten logic views such a move sacrilege ... defying the principles of selfish attachment ... dog in the manger territory ... and slowly their will to live again flickers and dies ... just like other dreams ... and they are seen no more ... forever consigned to the land of broken promises ... in their very own leather graveyard.

The inevitable chat ensued, with tea replaced by vino, wherein Julie was on Charlie's side, while Marianne agreed that whereas she did love the poem, and possibly still loved him, she still had huge problems with the position she now found herself in and the part Charlie played in getting her there.

…the walls are closing in…

Marianne arrived back at 125 West St in the dark on a late Friday night flight, keeping a low profile. After a fitful night's sleep, she awoke with a splitting headache and a frantic search through her bag revealed that she had left her medicine at her aunt's, and it was yet another one of the wettest imaginable Saturday mornings in Dunstable. She needed something for the headache but she really didn't want to use the car Ricki had bought for her, so she hoped that tea and toast would work. But it didn't, so she felt there was only one thing for it, to head to the pharmacy in the same shopping centre as before. In total irony, she felt the heavy rain would shelter her.

On the return to the car, the driving rain meant she did not see two of the guys she often saw with Ricki standing nonchalantly beside the car till it was too late. Her first instinct was to pretend she was heading for the bus, as if she knew nothing about the car, but they quickly blocked her path, as one remarked,

'Ricki tells me that on one of the first times he met this woman, it was here in this very shopping centre. Apparently she resembled a wet rat scurrying towards an overfull bus in the rain, and will you look at her now, driving in style and not long back from a little holiday.'

Marianne instinctively knew it was safer for her to remain silent.

He continued with the rehearsed conversation.

'And how do you think she shows her gratitude? By splitting her benefactor's eye wide open. And while he was having serious surgery and is being told he will probably never see from that eye again, she was arranging a secret tryst in Ireland with her former lover.'

Here the other guy joined in the choreographed chat between the two. 'You mean the father of that crying child we bundled into the car that morning?'

Nodding, the other guy approached Marianne, laughing.

'The very one!' He then looked intensely at her. 'Seems you owe our friend big time.'

She looked around for some outdoor cameras.

'Sorry love, we've already checked. Now, hand over the car keys,' he demanded.

Her hands were shaking as she fumbled in her handbag and tried to remove her front door key from the keyring. Of course they fell onto the ground in the rain, which was a source of great amusement to the two. When she finally managed to do so, he took them and tossed them to the other guy, silently indicating instruction to him, before addressing Marianne.

'Now, get the bus home, the same bus poor Ricki should have left you on in the first place, you ungrateful bitch.'

Then, in a potentially dangerous turn, his mate spoke up.

'I have a better idea. Why don't we bring her home, and she can find a way of thanking us when we get there.'

Thankfully, the other guy suddenly took control.

'Leave it! Ricki said she's his, that he'll deal with her himself.'

As the two sped away in the car she had arrived in, Marianne began shaking and now knew precisely what Charlie had experienced on the fateful morning that Mary Elizabeth had been snatched.

While she waited for the next bus, she thought over two things, her sheer terror of Ricki being one, and the other being Charlie's words in the garden centre a week earlier. 'Whatever it is, I want to be involved. I want to help. I owe you.' She would take Charlie up on his offer to help and ask him to fly over to Luton to help her return to Ireland in a little over a week's time.

On the following Monday morning, she went to the nearby travel agent and organised tickets for Charlie's trip over on Friday next and both tickets back to Dublin on the following morning. She placed Charlie's ticket in an envelope with a brief letter, thanking him for his kind offer, without giving him the exact date of the return flight. Her situation was now crucial and if he meant what he'd said, he would surely help her.

…end of the line…

As Charlie got off the plane in Luton on the following Friday night and saw Marianne waiting for him, he experienced such a variety of feelings, but mostly a strong feeling of redemption.

He was aware that Marianne's request to come help her return to Ireland was couched in the *as friends* bracket but that was ok. And even if he had noticed perhaps a hint of desperation about her decision to return to Ireland, and even if she seemed totally distracted when they last met, Charlie felt there was nowhere else he would rather be in this moment.

But when she told him that she had a return flight booked for the morning, he did feel disappointed.

'To be honest, I was hoping we could spend tomorrow together and return home on Sunday,' he said.

But her voice took on an urgency as she told him that sometimes things are better done quickly.

On the bus journey from the airport, Charlie wondered what it would be like to see the house again, to feel welcome there again, to spend a night there again. And he wondered why they were taking a bus instead of a taxi but decided not to raise it.

And when they got inside 125 West St, she held him in the longest hug he had ever experienced, apart from the hug his mother had given him when he was leaving for the monastery. Again Charlie sensed the hug to be of the holding on variety rather than anything romantic and wondered for the first time what exactly was going on. But he was with Marianne and that was enough for now.

'I love my new job,' he told her in an attempt to ease the tension, 'it even has a company car. And I'm definitely going to complete my professional training as a counsellor. It's a career that I think I'd both love and be good at.'

'I'm happy for you,' she said. 'I'm going to live with my Aunt Julie and work in her art & craft shop.'

Charlie knew that his enthusiasm at this point was way out of sync with Marianne's worry but couldn't help himself.

'Will we be able to meet up like before?'

'Is it ok if we talk about us when we get to Ireland?' she asked.

'Of course,' he said, 'of course. Is there anything you'd like to do tonight, or have you to pack?'

'No. I packed all I need earlier.'

'Would you like to go for a walk?'

'I'm sorry,' she said, 'but Uncle Robert has organised a brief workplace goodbye tonight, and I can't really refuse.'

'Of course. You must go.'

He noticed that when the housephone rang, Marianne jumped. It was Robert to say he was busy and wondering if it would be possible for her to get a taxi to the work-do venue. Again, Charlie couldn't help but notice the panic in her voice as she pleaded with Robert to collect her, to which he eventually agreed.

Suddenly she turned to Charlie.

'Will you come with me, please?'

Charlie was beginning to see that all was not what it should be but was still not clued in quite enough to fully understand her request.

'I so appreciate the invite, but it's your night. It'll only take the focus off you if you have to introduce me to everyone.'

Marianne reluctantly could see his point.

So, when Robert arrived, she once again hugged Charlie goodbye in a *wish I didn't have to go* kind of hug. There was so much she would like to tell him, and she would, once they set foot back in Ireland. For now, she was glad he was here. He told her take her time and watched her through the window as she got into Robert's Mercedes.

But his concerns for her quickly vanished. Charlie already had his own plan for the evening, but it would have been unfair to wreck her pretty head with all that now. There'd be lots of time tomorrow for her to tell him all about her night, and for him to tell her all about his own mission.

The one thing that had kept him going since he had last been here was the thought that someday he would return and repeat his school walk of that fateful morning, knowing that the experience this time would be a much more peaceful one, with a redemptive closure.

Ideally, he would have liked to have retraced that walk with Marianne, but as they would be leaving in the morning, he would do so alone. For this walk was really important to him, and it was very unlikely she would be home before him. And it would be nice for him to take in the whole of the town he'd had neither time nor appetite for in his last such walk.

Happy with that rationale, as he noticed the irony of the rain, he pulled the door of 125 West St behind him, and glad he was wearing a good raincoat, Charlie headed out into the fading light and began to walk.

Each step was more therapeutic than the one before it and he never felt as peaceful as he did in that moment. Suddenly the town of fear from his memory had transformed into one of bright lights and lively atmosphere, and Charlie's mood matched it all. There was something about walking in the rain, he thought.

Sooner than expected, walking alone being much faster than taking a reluctant child to school, he reached the exact location where the events of that horrible morning had occurred. He had planned to savour this moment, so he sat peacefully on the garden wall that had held him upright on that morning and allowed himself the luxury of enjoying the journey from trauma to therapy. But from nowhere, a rush of fear gripped him, a strong fear that Marianne might not be ok, as he realised he had not paid sufficient attention to the fact that she seemed very preoccupied both at the airport and since. Was it possible she was afraid of someone or something and he had not been listening as well as he should have been?

He found a public phone box. Luckily, Marianne had given him some English coins at the airport, 'just in case'. He called her landline, but as it rang out, he realised that she wasn't of course at home, so he left a really loving voicemail, stating that he fully respected their friends status, but was very much looking forward to both of them being on the same side of the Irish Sea for a change. Even that action calmed him and he realised that his worry was probably all in his head.

As tends to happen at such events, the goodbye bash for Marianne went on way too long. Uncle Robert had really meant well in fairness and comforted her by assuring her that whenever it ended, he would bring her home. He could not have known that it was the worst night for something like this as far as an increasingly anxious Marianne was concerned. But she could not be rude, so the night stretched on till a point came where she said she had better call Charlie. She was happy to see a pay phone in the premises and called her own landline, but it just rang out, as happened again after a half hour, and an hour later.

She eventually got to say a final goodbye to Robert and her work colleagues, then Robert drove her home. When she saw the house lights on at 125 West St, she felt relieved.

'I'm home,' she announced when she walked in the door. But there was no response. She quickly closed the door and locked it before going upstairs as she called Charlie's name out loud. But he was not there. Immediately thoughts of déjà vu resurfaced, so she went back down to the kitchen to search for a letter. But there was no letter. And there was no Charlie.

…should have known better…

It was an hour later, there was no sign of Charlie and Marianne was beginning to feel sick.

She thought Charlie must have decided to go out, but if so, where to and why at this hour of night? She was glad that she had given him a key, so she comforted herself by thinking he might just have gone to the nearby pub to watch some sport. But, in this, she knew she was grasping at straws as she tried to calm herself.

The stark fact was that Charlie was not home. On the off-chance he had been phoning, she decided to check the message minder on her landline. Hearing his message and checking the timing of it, she felt even more worried. Why wasn't Charlie home? What, or more worryingly, who could have delayed him? In her rising panic, she felt she had no option but to call Robert again. Thankfully, he was home and answered. Sensing her panic, he assured her he would be there in ten minutes. She felt better at that, knowing she would not be alone. No doubt, it would all prove to be nothing. There would be a simple explanation, and they would have a good laugh at it all tomorrow. But right now, it didn't feel that way.

Then she heard a noise at her front door and thought Robert can't be here already, so thank God, it must be Charlie. But, before she could get out of her chair, she heard the noise of something dropped through the letter-box and a car driving off at high speed. Not knowing who had dropped it and what it might be, her now terrified mind went into overdrive.

And even when she recognised the sound of Robert's car, her fear was such that she was slow to open the door to him. When she eventually did, she found herself stepping on something which Robert was bending down to pick up, and Marianne remembered her previous visitor.

'Be careful, Robert,' she urged but he, not knowing the context, simply opened it. It was a CD and a scribbled note in block capitals: *SEE TRACK 2.*

Track two was "I should have known better" by Jim Diamond.

…A reason to remember…

In the renewed calmness that followed his leaving that voicemail to Marianne, Charlie was aware of the uniqueness and preciousness of this moment, a moment to savour, the apex of his redemption. He allowed himself to immerse in this sacred place of peace with his past, indulging in the moment while excited about what might lay ahead. In this space, he thought about life in general and how for some unlucky people, redemption moments like this never happen, as he felt a tremendous sense of gratitude.

Recalling memories of that last walk with his child to school served its purpose well for Charlie. It was very much as he had hoped, and it felt good. But the memories seemed to take on a life of their own, as if the events of that terrible morning were slowly, weirdly, becoming live on a giant screen in front of him.

At the point in the film where the two cars mounted the footpath, Charlie could actually hear tyres screeching, but here the film seemed to drift back to reality as a black van replaced the two cars. Then it was as if the film dovetailed with reality again as masked men ran towards him and quickly overpowered him.

But there was no child, so why was all this still happening? He was to find out when he felt a bag being forced over his own head, his hands and legs tied and he was being bundled into the back of the van.

After an extremely short but fast journey, Charlie was manhandled into some kind of barn, where he was left alone with only his thoughts for company. He had no idea what all of this was about and felt sure he was the victim of some kind of mistake.

Everywhere became dangerously quiet. After what seemed the longest time, he heard the barn door open and quickly close.

Then that distinguished accent he had such good reason to remember from his daughter's kidnapping.

'Charlie, remember me?'

'In the situation I'm in, it's not the worst voice I could hear.'

'Why is that, Charlie?'

'You can clear up what is clearly a mistake.'

'A mistake?'

'I haven't done anything. Even under police interrogation after that morning, I refused to give any details about ye guys.'

Ricki gave kind of a sad laugh. 'I take it you have no idea why you're here.'

'It's obviously a case of mistaken identity.'

'No mistake, Charlie, no mistake.'

'It has to be.'

'Let me explain, Charlie. The last time I encountered you and your child, you were living here with a lady.'

'What about her?'

'Let's just say that I know you two have plans to spend the rest of your days living the dream back in Ireland.'

'And what business of yours would that be?'

'I'll tell you what business it is, shall I?'

Ricki pulled the bag from Charlie's head and shoved his heavily bandaged face really close to Charlie's.

'That's the business it is, Charlie. Look what she's done to me.'

Charlie's face showed a look of complete innocence.

'You really don't know, do you?' Ricki said.

Charlie shook his head in bewilderment.

'That crazy bitch hasn't told you?'

'Told me what?'

'The pretty Lady Marianne tried to destroy me, and pretty much succeeded. Apart from half blinding me, I could easily have bled to death.'

Charlie kept calm. 'You're lying. She doesn't know you or anything about you. I told no one about the details from that morning.'

'That's where you're wrong, Charlie.'

'How?'

'You'd better ask her, Charlie. You seem blind to the facts, if you'll excuse the unfortunate pun. Let me help you out here. Your beloved Marianne has been my lover for the past two years and more.'

On this revelation, Charlie felt his stomach heave, as he exhausted his last desperate attempt at denial.

'You're deluding yourself.'

'For sure, one of us is deluding themselves, and it's not me.'

Ricki took a cassette tape from his pocket and placed it alongside a cassette-player on a bench.

'You can listen to it yourself later.'

'Listen to what?'

'A recording of your dream woman in the full flow of her first bedtime encounter with me. It's all there on that tape, Charlie. You'll very definitely recognise her voice and mine at various stages of that incredibly passionate hotel encounter. I've had many women in my day, Charlie, but Marianne leaves them all trailing in her wake.'

'Please, let me go,' Charlie pleaded. 'As you've said yourself, I'm a completely innocent party in all of what's happened to you.'

'I do feel for you, Charlie, but I can't allow someone who has disfigured me to get away with it. Surely, Charlie, even you understand that's not my way.'

'But I had nothing at all to do with it,' Charlie continued to protest.

'An eye for an eye, Charlie. Now, I could simply have chosen her, or you, or in fact both of you, but that would have been too easy. So, I've come to a decision. One of you

187

pays. The other suffers silently in guilt for the rest of their life. Good, isn't it. But which will it be?'

Charlie's body seemed to detect that he was in severe danger as his breathing became noticeably laboured.

'Apparently you both had a great love of the film *Sophie's Choice*. Well, that film theme has helped my decision.'

Charlie's breathing suddenly changed from laboured to almost being non-existent, as Ricki shared what he called his genius decision.

'I won't decide who pays, Charlie. You will.'

Charlie's voice was low. 'What do you mean?'

Ricki's voice took on a horrible tone as he rose.

'You know damn well what I mean, Charlie. I'll leave you think about it during the long night ahead as you listen to that tape, no doubt over and over and over.'

Charlie made one last-gasp request. 'Can you at least untie me?'

Ricki took out a knife and walked very slowly behind where Charlie was sitting, causing Charlie to stiffen, waiting for the inevitable pain.

But, to his relief, Ricki instead began cutting the ties from his hands and legs.

'Absolutely, Charlie, absolutely. And I'll allow you a good night's sleep by not putting that smelly bag back over your head.'

Charlie was by now less fearful but perhaps more confused.

'And the good news gets even better, Charlie. I'm not even going to lock the door, but of course me or the boys will be doing a few spot checks before morning.'

In his confused state, Charlie retreated to a childlike viewpoint.

'I can't stay here. There's nothing to sleep on.'

'Charlie, I think you have plenty to sleep on, don't you?'

THE END

Acknowledgements

I would like to acknowledge Ms Madeline Nugent Polcer for her wonderful cover art, Mark Turner of Marble City Publishing for his editing and layout work, and all those who have encouraged, supported and in any way helped the creation and completion of this book.

www.ingramcontent.com/pod-product-compliance
Lightning Source LLC
Chambersburg PA
CBHW031234260626
47169CB00007B/2283